P9-DNF-664
3 1804 00216 2566

THE ADVENTURES OF JACK LIME

By James Leck

KCP Fiction is an imprint of Kids Can Press

Kids Can Press acknowledges the financial support of the Government of Ontario, through the Ontario Media Development Corporation's Ontario Book Initiative; the Ontario Arts Council; the Canada Council for the Arts; and the Government of Canada, through the BPIDP, for our publishing activity.

Published in Canada by
Kids Can Press Ltd.
29 Birch Avenue
Toronto, ON M4V 1E2

Published in the U.S. by
Kids Can Press Ltd.
2250 Military Road
Tonawanda, NY 14150

www.kidscanpress.com

Edited by Karen Li
Designed by Karen Powers
Spot illustrations on cover and interior pages adapted from images © istockphoto/A-Digit/marlanu/johnwoodcock

Printed and bound in Canada

This book is printed on acid-free paper that is 100% ancient-forest friendly (100% post-consumer recycled).

CM 10 0 9 8 7 6 5 4 3 2 1
CM PA 10 0 9 8 7 6 5 4 3 2 1

Library and Archives Canada Cataloguing in Publication

Leck, James
The adventures of Jack Lime / written by James Leck.

ISBN 978-1-55453-364-0 (bound). ISBN 978-1-55453-365-7 (pbk.)

I. Title.

PS8623.E397A64 2010 jC813'.6 C2009-903923-0

Kids Can Press is a Corus™ Entertainment company

For Heather, who believed when I didn't, who picked me up when I was down, and who kept me writing when I wanted to stop. And for Zoe and Isaac, remember to follow your dreams.

A NOTE FROM THE AUTHOR

What you are about to read are some of the more interesting cases that have crossed my desk. You see, I'm a detective, a private investigator, a gumshoe. What I do is fix problems for people who need their problems fixed. My name is Jack Lime, and these are my stories.

THE CASE OF THE BROKEN LOCK

Friday, May 23, 3:25 p.m.
29A Main Street, The Diner

It was a hot and sunny day. The first hot and sunny day we'd had in Iona in nearly two weeks. The kind of hot and sunny that makes your shirt stick to your back. The kind of hot and sunny that makes the air thick and hard to breathe. The kind of hot and sunny that makes you daydream about running down to the river and jumping in with all your clothes on. All the other kids in Iona were outside, soaking up the heat like a bunch of lizards, but not me. I was inside, tucked into the rear booth of The Diner, where not even the rays of the sun could touch me, nursing a root beer float and trying to ignore my throbbing left eye as it swelled shut. The place was empty except for the owner, Moses, who was in the back clinking dishes together. Empty wasn't unusual for The Diner, a place with no real name, set back a little from all the other stores on Main Street. But empty suited me just fine. I needed a little peace and quiet. That's when Sandra Kutcher walked into my life.

Sandra was a tall twelfth grader, with long blond hair pulled back in a ponytail. She was wearing a pink T-shirt that had "Doll" printed on it in sparkly letters, a white skirt and a pair of flip-flops that slapped her heels when she walked.

"I'm looking for Jack Lime," she said, before the door had a chance to close behind her. My eye started to throb a little harder. Members of the social elite at Iona High had been hunting me down all day. When they found me, it always meant trouble. I figured Sandra was just another angry grad looking for a chance to pay me back for breaking up Iona High's Prom King and Queen a month before the big night. Just one more kid from the inner circle who wanted to pay me back for showing the world the truth. Well, sorry folks, but showing the world the truth is my job.

"I'm Jack," I muttered.

"Oh, thank God I found you!" she said.

I was waiting for a slap in the face or maybe a kick in the groin, so, "Oh, thank God I found you!" was not the reaction I was expecting.

I thought we were alone until she started toward my booth, revealing a grim, ghostly boy standing in her shadow. He was short and doughy with a bowl cut of jet-black hair. He wore a plain white T-shirt, black jeans that were two sizes too short, white socks and shiny black dress shoes. All that black and white made him look like a triple-decker Oreo cookie. I wasn't even sure if Sandra knew he was back there until she slid into my booth and motioned him over with a wave. "Well, come on, Ronny," she said. "You're the reason we're here, after all." She waited for Oreo to join us, then leaned across the table and whispered, "They told me you find things out."

"Finding things out is how I got this," I said, pointing at my shiner.

"Oh," she said, sitting back in the booth. Even disappointed she was drop-dead gorgeous. "But you can, like, find things out, right?"

Sandra was the type of girl who made boys do stupid things, even boys who needed to take a long hiatus from finding things out. Her silky blond hair, her sparkling green eyes, her lips covered in pink gloss. If she had asked me to pour my float over my head, jump through the plate glass window at the front and fling myself in the river, I would have done it. Long story short, I was falling for her, and I was falling hard. I took a swig of my float, set the glass back on the table and wiped my mouth with my napkin. "You might be able to convince me."

"Ronny's bike was stolen last night, and it's his birthday tomorrow, and he loves that bike because he's had it, like, forever, so he really wants it back for his birthday, and if you could find it, that would be just super."

Oreo said nothing. He just sat twiddling his thumbs.

"Sounds like an interesting case," I said. I was lying, but it sounded less harmful than snapping pictures of the captain of the football team (the Prom King) holding hands with one of his linebackers. Plus, I was ready, willing and able to do anything for this dame, including making ridiculous promises. "I'll tell you what. I'll find that bike, and I'll get it to you by tomorrow, or I'll personally buy Ronny a new bike."

"Great!" she exclaimed, and started pushing Ronny out of the booth. They were halfway to the door when she turned back and added, "Oh, and by the way, Jack, can you get it to us by two? That's when Ronny's party starts. Thanks!" Then she was gone.

Was it possible to track down a missing bike in less than twenty-four hours in a town like Iona? Probably not, but I wasn't going to bore a girl like Sandra with anything as dull as "the facts" or "reality." She was the type of person who lived in a different stratosphere than the rest of us poor slobs. So I figured I'd better get cracking on the case.

I pushed the float away, slid out of the booth and headed for the door. I was just stepping outside when I realized I didn't know thing one about this case. I didn't know what the bike looked like. I didn't have a stinking list of suspects. I hadn't even asked a single solitary question. That's what Sandra did to me; she turned me into a slobbering amateur without a sweet clue how to investigate a case. I took a long breath, gathered my wits and marched back into The Diner. There was a pay phone on the back wall. I grabbed the phone book and flipped to K. Lucky for me there was only one Kutcher in town.

Friday, May 23, 3:56 p.m.
14 Mercury Lane, The Kutcher Place

Fourteen Mercury Lane was the typical brick-front split entry that infests this white-bread town we call Iona.

With its perfect lawn, tidy little garden and white picket fence, the Kutcher residence was just another paint-by-numbers suburban clone-home. I strolled down the walk and knocked on the front door. I have to admit, I didn't mind asking Sandra if she'd step outside to answer a few questions.

We all gathered in the driveway. Ronny stood off to the side, tracing imaginary lines on the ground with his shiny black dress shoes. Sandra stood beside me.

"Ronny always locked his bike to the fence," she said. She'd taken her hair out of the ponytail, and it hung in loose curls just below her shoulders. The way the sun was hitting her made her shine like an angel.

"Where exactly was it locked?" I asked.

She led me to the spot, and I took a close look at the fence. There was no damage to the wood or even to the paint.

"What kind of lock was it?" I asked.

"Just a regular lock," she said.

"A combination lock?"

"It was just a regular lock," she said in a tone that made me think she was getting annoyed by my questions, and when people get annoyed by my questions, I get interested. I learned at the school of hard knocks you can't cross anyone off your list of suspects, even if they're a dame and you've gone dizzy over them.

"One of those U-shaped locks?" I asked.

"Look," Sandra said, a flash of red in her cheeks, "we don't care about the lock. Ronny wants his bike back, not the lock, the bike! It's red with, like, a yellow banana seat, white streamers and a silver bell on the handlebars. We don't care about the lock. We can get a new one of those."

A kid that looked like an Oreo, riding around on a big yellow banana? The poor sap would have drawn less attention to himself riding a unicycle.

"Could I at least see the lock?" I asked, trying not to laugh.

"Why would we have the lock? They robbed us. Remember? Are you even taking this seriously, Jack?"

Before I had a chance to answer, Ronny spoke up in a voice so low he could've been singing bass in a barbershop quartet. "It was a U-shaped lock, with a blue plastic covering."

"What?" I asked, turning to the kid. Was he just pulling my leg with that voice?

"It had a blue plastic covering," he said again. This was no joke; Ronny's voice was deeper than a foghorn on the fritz.

"Were you the only one with a key?" I asked.

Ronny nodded.

"Do you know anyone who would want to steal it?"

"If we knew who wanted to steal the bike, we'd, like, go find them ourselves," Sandra said.

"Maybe the Riverside Boys took it," Ronny said, ignoring her.

"Ronny," Sandra said, walking over to him and putting her hand on his shoulder, "those boys are too big to be interested in your bike. They couldn't even ride it."

"But they could sell it," Ronny said, obviously getting excited about being involved in a real investigation.

"At the Flea Market," I added, with a smirk.

"Yeah," Ronny nodded. "They'd sell it at the Flea Market."

FYI — The Riverside Boys are a bunch of high school thugs who get their kicks stealing stuff from honest kids like you and me. Then they unload the merchandise down by the Iona River on Friday nights. They call their little business venture the Flea Market. Real classy.

"Sounds like a good lead," I said, flashing Ronnie a "good thinking, kid!" kind of smile. But I had serious doubts that anyone, let alone the Riverside Boys, would get much on the black market for a bike with a yellow banana seat and streamers.

"No one would steal Ronny's bike to sell it," Sandra whispered, leaning close to me. "He got it for his seventh birthday, but he hasn't grown for, like, five years, so he can still ride it. He loves that bike so much that Mummy and Daddy can't bear to get him another one. But nobody else would want it. It's just some jerk out for a cruel joke."

She smelled like coconut sunscreen. I thought, for a brief moment, we made a real connection, but then it was gone. "Don't worry, Sandra," I whispered. "I'll find the bike, and I'll get it to you by two."

She smiled and squeezed my arm, sending the most pleasant electrical tingle through my whole body. "Let me know if you need anything else," she said. "Come on, Ronny, we have to set the table for supper."

I wandered down to the street and sat on the curb. I had less than twenty-four hours to find a bike that nobody in their right mind would want to steal. If I was going to crack this case, I had to stick to the facts:

1. Ronny's bike was stolen last night.
2. It was attached to the fence with a U-shaped lock.
3. The lock and the bike are gone.
4. Ronny loves his funny little bike.
5. Sandra's easy on the eyes.

(I couldn't help adding that last one. She really is a knockout.)

I walked back up the driveway and squatted by the fence where the bike had been locked. In my experience, and I've dealt with a few stolen bikes in my time, most bicycle thieves worth their salt would use liquid nitrogen to smash Ronny's lock to bits. It's easy, quick and quiet; you just dip the lock into the liquid nitrogen and then whack it with a hammer. The thing is, there's always chunks of metal and plastic left behind on the ground. Granted, it rained last night, but I'd still bet dollars to doughnuts there'd be a few pieces scattered here and there. But there was nothing, nada, *niet*. More importantly, if the perps smashed part of the lock or even if they used heavy-duty cutters, why would they take a broken lock with them? It was a small detail, but it bothered me.

All this speculation was adding up to bupkes, and I'm not a big fan of bupkes. The problem was I had nothing to work with except Ronny's crazy hunch that the Riverside Boys had swiped his bike to sell on the black market. It was probably a dead end, but it was something to go on, and I knew exactly who to talk to.

Friday, May 23, 4:27 p.m.
2 Ganymede Court, Iona Elementary

Missy King is Bucky King's little sister. Bucky is the Grand Poo-bah of the Riverside Boys. He's as big as an ox and twice as strong. He's the only kid in Iona who drives to school on a Harley, the only student who's taller than all of the teachers at Iona High and the only person I've ever seen who can smoke a cigarette and dunk a basketball at the same time. I couldn't just wander over to Bucky and ask him about stealing Ronny's dinky little bike without risking my life, but I could ask Missy. She owed me one.

FYI — Here's how my P.I. business works; you come to me with a problem like, "I think my boyfriend, the quarterback of the football team and the King of the Prom, is cheating on me. Can you follow him around and find out?" So I follow him around for three days, hiding in garbage cans and sneaking around in locker rooms until I find out he is cheating on you, and then you owe me one favor. I steer clear of cash because I learned the hard way that things can get very messy when you're dealing with dough. So I charge by the favor instead. For instance, the Queen of the Prom now owes me one favor, and it's going to be a doozy, because her boyfriend, or should I say ex-boyfriend, is the reason I'll be seeing the world out of one eye for a few days.

Missy owes me a favor, too. I helped her out of a tight jam about a month ago. Ms. Crenshaw accused her of stealing the marking sheet for a big math test. She was just about to get tossed out of school when I saved her bacon by proving it was Ben Snider all along. It had to do with some missing lunch money and a pair of dirty socks, but that's another story.

"Hi, Missy," I said, approaching the playground. Missy is built like an Olympic gymnast; short, but rippling with hidden power. She was hanging upside down on the monkey bars, her pigtails pointing at the ground like a couple of horns.

"Lime," she said, flipping off the bars and stamping toward me.

"I'm calling in my favor," I said, stopping her in her tracks.

She didn't answer. She just looked me up and down and smacked her gum a little harder.

"I'm looking for a bike."

"I didn't have nothing to do with it."

"So, you know something about a bike that's been swiped?"

"I didn't have nothing to do with it. Bucky took it. I tried to take it back."

"Don't make it hard on yourself," I said. "Just tell me where the bike's at."

"You calling me a liar?" she asked, jutting out her chin.

"I don't have time for your cat-and-mouse games, Missy. Tell me where I can find that bike."

"I tried to bring it back, but the stupid kid had a new one."

I ignored this. Missy is like the devil; she'll mix her lies with the truth. "Where's the bike?" I demanded again.

Without warning, she sprang across the few feet that separated us and kicked me, kung fu–style, in the stomach. I crumpled to my knees, winded. Tiny black dots floated in front of me, and the world tilted. Through a haze, I saw her bolt across the playground.

I was having the second-worst day of my life; I'd been called a liar (even though I have the pictures to prove everything), I'd been beaten up by the quarterback of the football team and now I'd been flattened by a little girl. I figured it might be best just to lie on the ground and flop around like a fish out of water. But since when did I do what was best for me?

I heaved myself up, staggered across the playground and caught a glimpse of Missy's pigtails bobbing up and down on the other side of a fence as she raced across someone's backyard. Unfortunately, just as I was pulling myself onto the fence, my condition kicked in.

FYI — My condition makes me fall asleep at the worst times. I can't help it. The doctors say it's neurological, which means there's something wrong with my brain. The shrinks say it's all in my head, but not in my brain. The shrinks say it's because I haven't come to terms with my parents dying. I say I've come to terms with it all right — as much as a kid can come to terms with a thing like that — but I still can't help falling asleep. They tell me to meditate, to exercise, to try and stay relaxed. But when you just got your butt kicked and you're jumping over a fence trying to catch the prime suspect in a robbery investigation, it's hard to stay relaxed. So my condition kicked in, and I fell asleep.

I dreamed I was lying on the bottom of the river. A purple grizzly bear rode up to me on a bicycle. He rang a bell on the handlebars, but it didn't make any noise.

Instead, a school of little fish, with sharp little teeth, came out of the bell and attacked me like piranha on the prowl. I tried to fight them off. I tried to bat them away, but I was tired, so tired. And that's when the bear got off the bike, waddled over and sat on my face.

I woke up gasping for air, but all I got was a mouthful of fur — cat fur, to be exact. A fat orange and white cat had decided to take a nap on my face while I was passed out. I swatted it away, sat up and checked my watch. Ten minutes had passed. Missy was long gone. I plucked cat hair out of my mouth and decided to head back to the Kutchers'.

Friday, May 23, 5:35 p.m.
14 Mercury Lane, The Kutcher Place

Standing on the Kutcher front stoop, I replayed what Missy had said. A bike had been snatched; there was no doubt about that. I didn't know where she was going with the whole "I tried to bring it back, but the stupid kid had a new one" spiel, but I had a hunch it was a smoke screen to keep her out of trouble. One thing I was pretty sure about — if the Riverside Boys had a hot bike, they'd be bringing it to the Flea Market tonight.

"Oh my God, Jack!" Sandra gasped, opening the door and breaking my train of thought. "What happened to your face?"

"Huh?" I said. I leaned to the side and caught a glimpse of my reflection in the window beside the door. I was covered in tiny scratches. The killer fish in my dream suddenly made sense; that cat must have been playing with my handsome mug before he decided to use my face as a bed. "Oh that. It's nothing," I said. The last thing I needed was for word to get out that the local P.I. fell asleep when the going got tough. "You got a minute?"

"Well, we're just starting supper," Sandra said, peering back into the house. "You can come in, but it'll have to be quick." She had changed out of her skirt and was wearing a pair of old gray sweatpants. It didn't matter; she was still out of this world.

"Is Ronny around?" I asked, slipping into the foyer. Somewhere in the house forks and knives tapped against plates.

"Just a sec," she said, gliding up the stairs and disappearing into a side room.

When she returned, she had a wet cloth and Ronny. He was still in his Oreo outfit (minus the dress shoes), which was made even more priceless by the white napkin tucked into his shirt collar.

"Thanks," I said, taking the cloth and wiping my face. "I've got some news about the bike."

"You found it," Sandra chirped, rising up on her toes and clapping her hands. This was very cute stuff.

"Not exactly," I said. "But I did find out that Bucky King and his merry band of hooligans are probably unloading a bike tonight at the Flea Market."

"What does that mean?" Sandra asked.

"It means that yours truly will be crashing the Riverside Boys' party tonight, and I'll find out if it's Ronny's bike."

"Won't that be dangerous?" Sandra asked.

"Yes, it will," I said, not mincing words. "It's going to be incredibly dangerous, but you're my client, and I'm willing to take that chance."

Sandra took my hand and looked deep into my eyes. "Be careful, Jack." We were having one of those moments between two people where the world stops and a classic love song kicks in, and you just melt into each other like two hot sticks of butter.

"Yeah, be careful!" Ronny boomed from the stairs, totally interrupting our romantic interlude.

"Find his bike, Jack," Sandra said, squeezing my hand, and then she went up the stairs and gave her brother a hug. "Don't worry, Ronny. Jack will get your bike back."

I let myself out.

Friday, May 23, 6:28 p.m.
A street with no name, Grandma's House

I had a plan. I was going to stake out the Flea Market, go undercover and infiltrate the Riverside Boys. This would be cloak-and-dagger stuff, and like any good snooper, I had a stash of top-secret paraphernalia that would get me into places that I wasn't supposed to get into. So I headed home to get my disguise together, check in with Grandma and grab a bite to eat.

Grandma was sitting in her rocking chair, knitting something red and watching *Jeopardy* when I slunk in through the front door.

"Sorry I'm late," I said, sitting on the couch. "I got caught up in a case." I made sure I had my black eye turned away from her. Grandma wasn't a spring chicken anymore, but she was as sharp as a tack. On top of that, she was a big lady. Not fat, just big. She was tall, with thick arms and wide shoulders. But what stood out the most were her hands; they were large and calloused from working in the garden (which was really more like a farm). In short, she wasn't someone you wanted to fuss with.

"What is the Ganges River," she said. On TV, a short man wearing a bow tie answered "the Nile" and got it wrong.

"People today don't know their geography," she said, shaking her head. "Now what were you saying, Jack?"

"Sorry I'm late," I said again.

"Off solving some great mystery, I suppose?"

"I don't know if I'd call it great," I said. "Just trying to find some kid's bike."

"Oh, they're all great mysteries, Jack. Even the small ones," she said without looking at me. "What is the Colorado River." This time the man with the bow tie agreed with my grandma and he got five hundred dollars richer.

"Anyway," I said, standing up and keeping my black eye out of sight, "I'll just grab something quick for dinner. I've still got a few loose ends to tie up tonight."

"There's meatloaf, potatoes and carrots on a plate in the oven, and a lemon meringue pie in the fridge."

"Thanks, Grandma," I said, moving toward the kitchen.

"Oh, and Jack," she called, without taking her eyes off the TV, "what's wrong with your eye?"

"What do you mean?" I asked, and kept walking.

"Halt!" she barked when I had one foot in the kitchen. She grabbed the remote control and pressed "Mute"; that's when I knew she was serious about having this conversation. I stopped and turned around.

"It's nothing, Grandma," I said. "I missed a fly ball in gym class."

"And all the scratches?"

"Looking for a foul ball in the woods behind the school," I said with a shrug.

Grandma frowned. We both knew this was a load of horse manure. She could smell it on me, but she couldn't prove it. Not that lying to my grandma was something I took pride in, but I'd heard plenty of stories about her rebellious younger years. I got the sense that she'd only be disappointed if I crumbled mid-bluff, so I held my ground under the gaze of her shrewd blue eyes.

"Gym class," she grunted.

"Gym class," I nodded.

"Curfew," she barked, "is ten o'clock sharp. You got that, young man?"

"I got it, Grandma," I said. Then the sound came back on the TV, and I slipped into the kitchen before she decided to call my gym teacher and check my alibi.

After I wolfed down some chow, I headed upstairs and got into character. I put on my disguise, which consisted of a blond wig, an old Cubs baseball cap and a black Nike hoodie. I managed to transform myself from the tall, dark and handsome Jack Lime you all know and love to my scruffy alter ego for the evening, Roger Daltry.

I topped off my new look with a pair of glasses that I'd found up in the attic. They were a little retro (in a Buddy Holly kind of way), and the prescription made things kind of blurry, but it wasn't anything I couldn't handle. Plus, I hoped they'd cover up my black eye a little, just in case Missy had let her brother know what I looked like. Now I was ready to get down to some serious business.

Friday, May 23, 8:57 p.m.
Riverside Park, The Flea Market

Riverside Park is a green belt that runs along the Iona River. The planners at Luxemcorp must've thought it would be just terrific for business if the fine citizens of Iona could sit on their patios, leisurely sipping cappuccinos, gazing across the river at the peaceful sway of the trees and listening to the gentle flow of the water. I hated to rain on their parade, but it wasn't all sunshine and lollipops on the other side of those trees, because every Friday night at nine, the Riverside Boys were getting ready to do some crooked business at a little something called the Flea Market.

I hunkered down behind some bushes with a good view of the trash-infested clearing the Riverside Boys used for their illicit business venture. The sun was just about to set, but here in the trees, it was already getting dark. The air was thick, and thanks to all the rain we'd been getting, it reeked of dampness. Farther down the river, ordinary people joked about the ordinary things they did in their ordinary lives. Here, at the far end of the park, an assortment of Iona's shadiest kids were setting up shop, ready to sell their wares to anyone with enough dough to grease their dirty little paws.

I took off my retro glasses and tucked them into my pocket so I could actually see the seedy activities that were just heating up as kids started to trickle into the clearing. They stumbled over rocks and slogged through the thick, black mud that lined the river just to find a cheap deal. These were kids who got good grades, kids who never got into trouble, all handing over their allowances to buy things that'd probably been stolen out of their best friend's locker. I saw Joey McQueen buying some poor sap's PSP. Lily Jones laid down cash for a pink cell phone. Billy Patterson got himself a new MP3 player. I didn't spot a bike in the mix, but I couldn't be sure there wasn't one being kept out of sight for the big rollers. I had to get a closer look, but I couldn't just march out of the trees like a guy busting in on his sister's pajama party. I had to be subtle about things.

I made my way back up to the main asphalt path that wound its way through the park and spotted the narrow trail that led to the market. I started down the path and went over the cover story I'd made for Roger. He was an out-of-town kid who'd heard the Flea Market was the place to be if you were looking for something cheap. His little brother was sick, so he wanted to get him something real nice for his tenth birthday. He was hoping to pick up a bike, maybe something with a banana seat and streamers. Everything was hunky-dory until I was ambushed halfway down the path.

"Freeze, buster! I got you covered!" someone shouted.

I whipped off the glasses and spun around, looking to see where the voice was coming from.

"I said freeze, bozo!"

"I'm just heading down to do a little shopping," I said. Was this some kind of security checkpoint the Riverside Boys had cooked up so they wouldn't be taken by surprise?

"State your name, soldier," the voice demanded. I thought I caught a glimpse of movement off to my right.

"Roger Daltry," I said. "I'm just looking for a bike for my kid brother."

"Just an innocent shopping trip, eh, Roger? Well, let me tell you something, the plan just changed."

Now I was sure the voice was coming from my right. I thought I could see a figure in the trees, and unless my eyes were playing tricks on me, that somebody was wearing an army helmet and his face was covered in green paint. The rest of his body was concealed behind a bush. I considered jumping into action, but didn't want to blow my shot at finding the bike if Sergeant Wingnut actually was a watchdog for Bucky's gang.

"Now listen carefully, soldier," he said. "You're going to march down that path and ask about a pair of night vision goggles. If they have them, you ask how much, and when they tell you, you act like you forgot your money. Then march back up here. Don't bother looking for me, just keep walking. I'll find you. And don't try to bail on me, bug-bait, because I'll be watching your every move. You got that?"

This wasn't a lookout from the Riverside Boys. This was a lone wolf cooking up some hare-brained scheme that would probably get me killed if I went along with it. I considered my options and decided to play along. I wanted to avoid any loud and messy confrontations.

"All right, boss," I said, in my best Nervous-Nellie voice. "I'll do what you want, just don't hurt me."

"Smart choice, soldier," he said. I could see him smiling beneath all that green paint. "Now hop to it!"

I left Private Nutso squatting in the woods and turned my attention back to the case. I had more important (and sane) things to do, so I straightened my wig, pulled down my hat and put on the glasses. It was showtime.

The path led me straight down to the clearing I'd been watching from the trees. I spotted three goons standing at the edge of the river and decided to see if they had the dope on this crooked operation.

"What's up, what's up, what's up, fellas?" I said, getting into character.

"What's up," the tallest one said. He had a sneer permanently frozen on his face. "You got any beer?"

"Afraid not, my man," I said. "I'm driving."

"So what?" Sneer said, and all three of them snickered like hyenas.

"You're not from Iona, are you?" another one of them asked. I recognized him from my geography class. He wasn't hard to ID because he had a head as big as a hot air balloon. But from what I'd seen in class, there wasn't much filling up all that space.

"No, I'm from out of town, but word is this is the place to go if you want a sweet deal on some high-end merchandise."

"So, how'd you get in?" Sneer asked.

FYI — Iona is a gated community, or an "insulated living environment," as the bigwigs at Luxemcorp like to say. There's an iron gate across the only road into town, and you need a security code to get it open. If you don't have the code, you have to get past the Luxemcorp guards who are posted in a little white house just inside the gate. Sneer was clearly testing my alibi, but I passed "Going Undercover 101" a long time ago, and these were silly kids' games.

"I parked on the highway," I said.

"Then you walked?" the third one asked. His name was Derek Sanders. Everyone calls him Heavy because he tips the scales at close to three hundred pounds, but couldn't be more than five foot eight. Heavy is also blessed with hair as red as a carrot, which makes him about as hard to spot as fireworks on the Fourth of July.

"That's right, chief," I said. "I needed the exercise."

"Whatever," Big Head grunted. "What are you looking for?"

"A bike," I said. "Something cheap, if you know what I mean."

"Yeah, I think I know what you mean," Heavy said, and winked at his compadres. Then he turned and disappeared into the trees.

When Heavy came back, he was wheeling a slick yellow and black mountain bike. It had heavy-duty wheels, shocks and lots of gears. This was not Ronny's bike. But at that particular moment, it wasn't the bike I was concerned about. It was the beast emerging from the trees behind the bike that got my attention. Sneer, Big Head and Heavy were intimidating in their own bungling kind of way, but this guy was tall and pumped up. He was wearing a plain white T-shirt, worn-out jeans and work boots that weren't laced up. He had one cigarette behind his right ear and another dangling between his lips as if it had been forgotten. This was Bucky King, in the flesh.

"Is this what you're looking for?" Heavy asked, stopping the bike in front of me. Bucky stood a few feet away and lit up his cigarette.

"Ah, actually, I was looking for something smaller," I said, trying to play it cool, "maybe with a few streamers, a banana seat and a little bell." I had to be careful; I didn't want to blow my cover.

"You're serious?" Sneer asked from off to the side. Big Head had disappeared.

"Yeah," I said, "it's for my little brother, Tommy. He's got a thing for streamers, banana seats and little bells."

"You must think I'm stupid," Bucky cut in, blowing a cloud of cigarette smoke into the air. "I don't suppose your little brother's last name is Lime? Tommy Lime? Is that his name?" he asked, stepping over to me and poking me hard in the chest with a massive finger. "'Cause I'm one hundred percent certain that you're Jack Lime. My sister told me you might be stupid enough to come down here tonight."

"You got me, Bucky," I said, holding up my hands. "You're a heck of a lot smarter than you look."

"Not really," Bucky said, completely missing my clever insult. "Because everything you've tried to pull tonight is so lame a retarded chicken could see through it."

"You're a long way from politically correct, my friend," I said.

"And you're a long way from Kansas, Dorothy." The small crowd that had gathered around us had a nice laugh at the expense of yours truly.

"Do you have the bike?" I asked, ignoring the fact that I was in no position to be asking questions.

Bucky smiled, started to turn away, then spun around and slammed his fist into my gut like a runaway locomotive. The wind blew out of me like a deflating balloon. I tried to crumple, but Big Head grabbed me from behind and held me up. "That's for my sister," Bucky said, and took a long drag from his cigarette. "I don't know what frigging bike you're looking for Lime, but you mess with me and you're going to pay."

"Do you ..." I said, sucking in air, "have ... the ... bike?"

"What bike, Lime?" Bucky said.

"Streamers ... banana seat ... little bell," I said, just starting to get my breath back. "Ronny ... Kutcher's."

"Kutcher? Sandra Kutcher's little brother?" he said. "Man, doesn't that kid still ride around on a tricycle?" The crowd laughed again. "Let me tell you something, Lime. Nobody's in the market for that kid's bike. That's small time. Real small time, and Bucky King ain't small time. And, Sandra, she ain't small time, either. She's a real sweet girl," he said, giving me a wink.

I stamped on Big Head's toes. He yelped, and I tried

to slip out of his grip, but he was too strong.

"Don't like that, Lime?" Bucky said, stepping close to me. "Well, you really ain't going to like this news flash, big man: me and Sandra used to hook up."

"I don't believe you," I said.

"It's true." Bucky grinned. "She couldn't get enough of me, but I had to break it off. She got kind of boring, a little needy. But I'll tell you, Lime," Bucky said, squeezing my cheeks into the kind of pucker my crazy Aunt April used to force on me when I was a little kid, "she was one hell of a kisser."

"I don't buy it, Bucky," I slurred through the pucker. "You're too ugly."

Bucky's eyes blazed, and he chomped down on his cigarette. I was sure another punch was on its way, but at the last moment, he stopped himself and stepped back. "Toss him in the river with the rest of the trash," he said, flicking the butt of his cigarette into the darkness. I watched the orange tip fly away and then sizzle in the black water of the Iona River. Big Head grabbed me around my chest, and Sneer grabbed my feet.

I kicked. I thrashed. I fought the good fight, and I wish I could tell you I escaped, but that would be a lie. They started swinging me back and forth, building momentum. "One ... two ... three!" they hollered. For a moment, I was flying through the air, and then I hit the water.

Bucky and his cronies thought this was all just fun and games. They'd toss me in the river, and I'd struggle out, soaking wet, with my tail between my legs, and never bother them again. Problem was they didn't know I was prone to falling asleep at the worst times. So a simple dip in the Iona River suddenly got very serious when I felt my condition kicking in. Just before I drifted off to Never-Never Land, I saw someone diving in the water, then everything went black.

I dreamed I was sitting on the bottom of the river. A purple grizzly bear rode by on Ronny's bike — banana seat, streamers and all. As he drove past me, he yelled, "Find the bike, Jack." I tried to say, "No thanks, bear," but my mouth filled up with water. That's when my dream took a turn for the worse. The purple bear was gone. Instead, I was staring into the face of a hideous green monster. It was descending on me, its mouth wide open, like it was going to bite my face off. I tried to scream, but choked instead.

"Oh, thank God," the monster said, leaning back. "I really didn't want to give you mouth-to-mouth."

That's when I realized this wasn't a dream. I wasn't under water; I was lying in the black mud on the banks of the river, with Colonel Crazy from the path kneeling beside me, apparently about to perform mouth-to-mouth resuscitation.

"I owe you an apology, soldier," he said. "I shouldn't have forced you into being my mole. But I didn't know that Bucky was going to go ballistic about a pair of night vision goggles. I mean, I know they're not easy to get your hands on, but that whole situation was seriously snafu."

"Not ... about ... the goggles," I said, coughing the words out.

"You know, soldier, I'm tired of all these good-for-nothing bums taking everyone's stuff and nobody doing anything about it," he said.

"It wasn't about ... goggles," I mumbled, starting to get my wits about me again.

"What's that, soldier?" he asked.

I sat up and finally got a good look at who I was dealing with. He was short and thin, with a wispy mustache growing behind the green paint covering his face. His helmet was gone, replaced by a short crew cut that still stood at attention even though it was soaking wet. He couldn't have been more than thirteen.

"You can relax," I said. "He didn't go ballistic about your goggles. It was over a bike."

"I told you to ask about the goggles, noncom," he said, getting a little testy.

"Yeah, well," I said, standing up and getting a little testy myself, "I'm in the middle of a case, so you'll have to do your own asking."

"What d'you mean, 'case'?"

"Case, assignment, investigation; call it whatever you want. But I've got a client who's counting on me to find a ridiculous bike, and you're barking at me about night vision goggles. Well, sorry, Sergeant Camouflage, but you're going to have to learn to do your own recon."

"What're you, like a detective or something?"

"That's right, smart guy."

"Say," he started, "we should work together. You could use someone like me. I got the drop on you on the path, after all, and I saved your bacon in the river. Plus, my dad's got loads of top-notch gear for undercover missions. What d'you say?"

"I say I'm done with this dirty gig, Major Pain, so you can have it all to yourself. Sayonara and good luck," I said, stumbling away.

"The name's Max," he called. "Max Thorn. Just give me a call the next time you need someone to save your butt, soldier!"

Friday, May 23, 11:38 p.m.
A street with no name, Grandma's House

My hat, my wig and my glasses had fallen off in the river. I'd been beaten up three times today, and worst of all, I'd just found out that Sandra had had a sordid fling with Bucky King. And what did I have to show for it? Nothing. I didn't even have a few coins to rub together. The way I figured, it was time to take down my shingle and take a permanent vacation from the P.I. business.

That's what I was thinking as I staggered home, so I didn't notice my grandma sitting on the porch as I stepped onto the front walk. I'd also forgotten about the ten o'clock curfew, and the fact that I was half-covered in mud.

"Burglar!" she yelled, grabbing the broom she used to sweep our porch. Unfortunately, Grandma didn't recognize the ragged stranger stumbling up her front walk, so she charged at me, waving the broom above her head like a helicopter warming up. Like I said, my grandma's not a small lady. So, I did the only thing I could think of; I ran. She would have woken up the whole neighborhood if we'd had any neighbors to wake up. As it is, my grandma lives on a deserted, dead-end dirt road without streetlights or even a name. She used to have neighbors until Luxemcorp bought up the town. My grandma and Moses (he owns The Diner) were the only two people who didn't sell out. Luxemcorp just built around them. So there I was, being chased down a deserted road in the middle of the night by my own grandmother. It was the perfect end to the perfect day.

"Grandma! It's me!" I yelled, but she didn't have her hearing aid in. We were halfway down the street when she clocked me in the head with the broom and knocked me to the ground. "It's me! Jack!" I yelled, rolling onto my back. She had the broom raised above her head, ready to drop the hammer on my noggin when she realized who I was.

"Jack," she growled, "you're late!" Then she turned, and without another word, marched back to the house.

While I grabbed a hot shower, got into a clean pair of pajamas and wrapped myself up in a dressing gown, Grandma warmed up some chicken soup. My eye was a stunning shade of purple and completely sealed shut, and my stomach felt like someone had driven over me with a truck.

"Jack," Grandma said, as I stepped into the kitchen, "I raised your father to have an inquisitive mind, and it served him well. But I'm a little worried about this detective agency you're running. Being late for dinner all the time or losing a few gadgets to some juvenile delinquents is one thing. Coming home in the middle of the night, soaked to the bone and covered in mud is another thing altogether."

"Technically," I said, sitting down at the kitchen table, "the middle of the night isn't until two or three in the morning."

"Cut the sass, Jack," she said, putting a steaming bowl of chicken soup in front of me and sitting down on the other side of the table. "When you got here in January, I knew I had to give you some space. Lord knows, you've had a rough go of it. And it can't be easy living out here with me, when everyone thinks I'm some kind of crazy old witch. But there's got to be a better way for you to make friends."

Make friends? If I hadn't been so tired and beaten down, I would have laughed in my soup. "Don't worry, Grandma. I've decided to quit the detective game for good."

"Smart boy," she said. "Why don't I call Moses on Monday and get you a proper job at The Diner?"

I started to agree, but she held up her hand. "No arguments. It's my way or the highway from now on, dear boy. Now, unless Your Majesty needs anything else, I'm going to hit the hay, and don't wake me up in the morning. I'm sleeping in."

Lying in bed that night, I decided to take myself off this case first thing in the morning. I'd been beaten up by a little girl, by Bucky and his buffoons and then by my own grandmother, all for a weird kid who dressed like an Oreo cookie and a dame. A dame who had a thing for Bucky King. The image of Sandra making out with Bucky burned in my mind. I won't lie, it hurt. It hurt bad.

Saturday, May 24, 9:26 a.m.
14 Mercury Lane, The Kutcher Place

Standing on the Kutcher front stoop, I promised myself I wouldn't mention Bucky. That was Sandra's private business, and as a professional, I wouldn't get involved in the private life of one of my clients. If Sandra wanted to make out with every lowbrow hood in Iona, who was I to stop her? Heck, if she wanted to go steady with every liar, cheat and dirty crook this side of Tokyo, be my guest. Far be it from me to stand in the way of true love. If she wanted to —

"Jack," Sandra said, opening the door and breaking my train of thought. "You don't look so good."

"It's nothing," I said, playing it cool, "nothing at all. Getting beaten up is just part of the job. I hardly notice it. It certainly didn't bother me last night. Not in the least. Even when Bucky was using my gut for boxing practice. You remember Bucky, don't you, Sandra? Bucky King?" To hell with professionalism and privacy; this was personal. "I believe you had a torrid love affair with him not so long ago!"

"Well —" she started, but I wasn't going to give her a word in edgewise. I was just getting warmed up.

"Bucky King! The guy who runs the Riverside Boys.

The guy who was the chief suspect in your burglary investigation. The guy who broke up with you! That Bucky King. Is this ringing any bells?" I was being cruel. I couldn't help it.

"Gosh, Jack," she said, "calm down. We went out for, like, two weeks in grade eight. I wouldn't exactly call it a love affair."

"Yeah," I said, "well ..." I was hoping for some yelling, some slamming doors, some passion, not, "Gosh Jack, calm down."

"So you don't have the bike?" she asked, trying to change the topic.

"Well ... but ... Bucky!"

"Do you think you'll find it before two? Ronny's really counting on you, Jack."

She was being so businesslike, so coldhearted. Well, if that's how she wanted to play it, I could play it that way, too. "That's why I'm here, Miss Kutcher," I said, staring her down with my one good eye. "I'm dropping the case."

"What?"

"I think you heard me loud and clear, toots. I'm out, finished, finito benito. I'm done with this gig for good. Next time you see me, I'll be just another sap washing dishes for a living."

"So you're, like, giving up?"

"That's right," I said. Our eyes met, and she knew no amount of eyelash batting or hand squeezing was going to change my mind.

"Well, you wait right here, Jack Lime, because you're breaking this to Ronny, not me." She darted up the stairs and turned down a side hallway, leaving the front door open.

What was with this dame? She just couldn't let it go. I was done like dinner, and she was practically begging me to stay on the case. Out of the corner of my eye, I caught a glimpse of her flip-flops lying just inside the door. Those were the ones she had worn when she drifted into my life. It seemed like only yesterday. I could remember how she looked, how she smelled, the way she smiled; it was making me weak. I had to stay strong, keep focused. I forced my eyes to the left and noticed Ronny's shiny black dress shoes. Beside his shoes was a pair of little sneakers caked in mud. They must've been Ronny's, too (unless Mr. Kutcher had extremely small feet). What kind of kid walks around in dress shoes instead of sneakers, even filthy sneakers? My own sneakers were covered in the thick black mud that lined the river, and you didn't see me gallivanting around town wearing my Sunday best. Heck, thanks to all the rain we'd been getting, every kid who'd been down to the river in the past two weeks had sneakers covered in that exact same black mud.

And that's when it hit me like a diamond bullet shot right through the middle of my forehead. I didn't wait for Sandra. I was back on the case.

Saturday, May 24, 9:44 a.m.
2 Ganymede Court, Iona Elementary

There were three things that had been bothering me about this case. One, why did the perp take the broken lock? Two, who in their right mind would want to steal Ronny's bike anyway? And three, what did Missy mean when she said she tried to return the bike, but the kid she was returning it to already had a new one? Obviously, the new bike she was talking about was the slick mountain bike that had been wheeled out last night just before Bucky laid into me, but who owned that bike? I had to pay Missy King another visit.

Missy was a creature of habit. I found her back at Iona Elementary, hanging upside down from the monkey bars.

"Missy," I called, standing back a bit from the playground equipment.

"What d'you want, Lime?" she said, hopping down. "More abuse?"

"I just need you to answer a question for me," I said.

"I don't owe you nothing anymore," she said, taking a few steps toward me.

"You're right," I said, taking a few steps back, "but I wonder how your brother would feel if he knew you'd tried to take some of his merchandise back to its rightful owner?"

"He wouldn't listen to a word you said," she said with a smirk.

"Probably not," I said. "But I don't have to tell him myself. I'd just have to call in a few favors, get a few people to start talking about how they saw Missy King riding around town on a new yellow and black mountain bike with heavy duty wheels and shiny shocks."

"How d'you know what it looks like?" she hissed.

I smiled. "I saw it last night. I might even get them to mention that the bike was stolen, and that it was up for sale at the Flea Market. Heck, I might even get someone to talk to Principal Snit about the whole messy affair."

"I'll rip you apart, Lime," she said, balling up her little fists and stamping toward me.

"A name," I said, holding my ground. "Just give me the name of the kid who owns the bike, and I'll keep my trap shut."

"A name?" she said, hesitating.

"That's all I want," I said, holding my hands up. "Then I'm out of your pigtails for good."

She frowned, then glanced around the empty playground. "Tommy Delane," she said. And then Missy did something I'd never seen her do; she blushed. "Now am-scray or I'm going to pull your eyebrows out."

She didn't have to ask me twice.

Saturday, May 24, 1:54 p.m.
14 Mercury Lane, The Kutcher Place

When I rounded the corner of the Kutcher house, Ronny's party was in full swing. Mr. and Mrs. Kutcher, Sandra, Ronny and a few of Ronny's friends (and when I say a few, I mean two) were standing around a purple piñata in the shape of a bear riding a bike. They were all clapping in rhythm. Ronny was spinning one of his friends around like a top. The kid was blindfolded and gripping onto a short wooden bat. When Ronny was done, the poor sap stumbled forward, fell on his face, tried to get back up and then fell down again. Mrs. Kutcher ran over and hoisted him up, but before she could clear out, the kid whacked her in the back of the legs with the bat. Mrs. Kutcher stumbled to the ground. Mr. Kutcher tried to get her away from the kid with the bat, but he got socked in the stomach. Sandra was yelling, "Stop!" and Ronny was laughing so hard, he nearly fell over. I ran into the chaos, just about got clobbered, then ripped the blindfold off the dumb lug. He looked like he'd just woken up from a terrible nightmare.

"What are you doing here, Jack?" Sandra demanded.

"Can I talk to Ronny for a second?"

"In case you hadn't noticed, we're, like, in the middle of a birthday party here."

"It'll only take a second."

Sandra frowned and huffed. "It better be quick," she said, squinting her eyes at me. "Come on, Ronny."

"What's going on, Sandra?" Mrs. Kutcher called, leaning on Mr. Kutcher for support. "We still have to break the piñata."

"It'll only take a second, Mummy," Sandra said, and the three of us retreated around the corner of the house.

"I thought you were off the case, Jack," Sandra hissed, as soon as we were out of sight.

"I need to speak with Ronny privately, Sandra," I said.

"No way!" she said, stamping her foot. "What you have to say to Ronny, you can say to me."

"Ronny," I said, ignoring Sandra, "I'd rather talk to you alone."

Ronny shook his head.

"It would be better if we spoke man to man, Ronny."

Ronny shook his head again.

"All right," I said, stepping away from the two of

them, "but remember, I tried to speak with you alone."

"What's this all about, Jack?" Sandra demanded.

"Follow me," I said, and led them to the front of the house.

There, leaning up against the white picket fence, was Ronny's old bike: banana seat, streamers and one silver bell.

"You found it! You found it!" Sandra squealed, jumping up and down, clapping her hands. Ronny walked to the bike and rang the bell. It emitted a squelching ring.

"I'm afraid it's still a little soggy, Ron, but it should be as good as new by tomorrow."

"Soggy?" Sandra said. "Where did you find it?"

"At the bottom of the Iona River," I said.

"You've got to be joking," Sandra said.

"Afraid not," I said. "It meant calling in three favors and borrowing half a dozen underwater masks, a fishing net and a U.S. Navy metal detector from a nut job who thinks he's in the Marines, but hang the expense! So long as Ronny here has his precious bike back for his birthday."

"How did you know?" Ronny asked. His face had gone from very pale to extremely pale.

"I'm glad you asked me that, Ron. You'll have to bear with me for a few minutes while I explain. You see, the first clue was the lock, or the fact that there was no lock. I wondered why anyone would break your lock and then take it with them. Why would anyone want a broken lock? Then I started to wonder who would be interested in your bike, but Sandra didn't think there was anyone interested in this particular bike —" I turned to Sandra, "— because it had certain special ... qualities. Ronny suggested the Riverside Boys took it and were planning to sell it at the Flea Market. I have to admit, that seemed like a long shot, but it was the only clue I had, so I followed it. That's how I ended up getting into a rather sticky situation with Missy King. But just before things got messy with Missy, she said something very interesting. She said she had tried to return the bike, but the owner already had a new one."

"What?" Sandra said. "Ronny doesn't have a new bike."

"Exactly," I said. "That's what confused me. So I chalked it up to one of Missy's outrageous lies to throw me off the trail. But clearly there was a bike that had been stolen, and it was going to be sold at the Flea Market. I didn't have any other clues to go on, so I decided to check it out just in case it was Ronny's. Turns out, the bike Missy was talking about was a brand-new twenty-one-speed mountain bike. I found out this morning it belonged to a kid named Tommy Delane. His bike was stolen about a week ago and he was all broken up about it. But his Dad has got some serious cabbage to spread around, so he went out and bought him a new one. Tommy just happens to be in Missy's class, and it didn't take a whole lot of digging to find out that she's got a major crush on the poor guy. So that's why she decided to return the bike and risk getting her knees broken by her big bro, Bucky. But, like I said, Tommy already had a new bike, so Missy took the old one back before Bucky had a chance to find out it was even missing. I didn't find out the bike Bucky had wasn't Ronny's until I was getting better acquainted with Bucky's hairy knuckles." I resisted giving Sandra one of my patented icy glares. "But, like his sister, Bucky said something very interesting just before we had to say good-bye. He said, 'Throw him in the river with the rest of the trash.' At the time, I wasn't in any condition to reflect on what he meant. However, today, when I came to tell you I was off the case, I noticed Ronny's muddy sneakers, and it all came together like one of my grandmother's patchwork quilts. And that's how I found your bike."

"What?" Sandra said. "That's it? I don't understand. What do Ronny's muddy sneakers have to do with anything?"

I looked over at Ronny, who was still standing beside the bike, but he didn't look back. "Good question, Sandra. Normally, a pair of muddy sneakers isn't a big deal. Heck, there're a lot of kids in Iona walking around in muddy sneakers right now. But you've got to ask yourself, how did they get muddy?"

"There're lots of places they can get muddy," Ronny said in a low growl.

"That's right, Ron. There are a lot of places they can get muddy, but your sneakers are so covered in mud that you've been wearing your dress shoes around. You're wearing them right now." I pointed to Ronny's feet. "I'd bet dollars to doughnuts he's been wearing those dress shoes since Friday morning."

"That's right!" Sandra said. "Mummy won't let him wear his sneakers until he cleans them up. They got in a big fight about it."

"So, how'd they get so dirty? Well, we've been getting

so much rain that anyone who's been down by the river would get their shoes covered in mud."

"Wait a minute," Sandra said, her eyes growing wide. "You don't mean ..." She couldn't finish. She just stared at her brother.

"That's right," I said. "There's no need to break the lock if you've already got the key."

"Oh, all right," Ronny said. "I did it! I took my stupid bike down to the river, and I rolled it in! I hate that bike! I hate it! I don't care if you all think it's great and how I've had it forever and ever and how Dad fixed it all up for me, just like I wanted it! It's stupid and it's slow and the other kids make fun of me for it! If I just got rid of it, I thought I'd get a new bike! And I would have, if it wasn't for this stupid face!" Ronny was crying and pointing one pale little finger right at me.

"Oh, Ronny," Sandra said, running to him and giving him a hug. Ronny buried his face in her shoulder and sobbed.

I risked my neck for this kid, and he's the one getting the hug. Typical.

"What's the matter, big guy?" Mr. Kutcher asked, coming around the corner of the house.

"It's nothing, Daddy," Sandra said.

"Is this your old bike?" Mr. Kutcher asked, walking over to the fence. "I thought it was stolen."

"Not exactly," I said. Sandra and Ronny turned and glared at me. I could finally see the family resemblance.

"Well," Mr. Kutcher said, pulling a garage door opener from his pants pocket. "I guess you won't be wanting this, then." The garage door opened, revealing a brand-new twenty-one-speed mountain bike.

"Golly!" Ronny said, running to the bike.

"A new bike! A new bike!" Sandra was jumping up and down again, clapping her hands.

"And just in time for summer," Mr. Kutcher added.

Saturday, May 24, 7:57 p.m.
29A Main Street, The Diner

It was a dark and stormy night. Good weather never seems to last very long around here. Every other kid in Iona was down the street at The Bijou catching a flick, or sucking down a mocha cappuccino at Monty's Cafe, or maybe locked in their room getting ready for final exams, but I wasn't. I was inside, tucked into the rear booth of The Diner, nursing a root beer float and trying not to think about Sandra Kutcher. The place was empty except for the owner, Moses, who was behind the counter sipping a hot cup of joe and listening to the Cubs game on his beat-up transistor radio. Empty wasn't unusual for The Diner, a place with no real name. Empty suited me just fine. I needed a little peace and quiet.

THE CASE OF THE DAILY TELEGRAPH

Monday, June 2, 8:26 a.m.
2 Pluto Court, Iona High

Gregory Pepperton, my client, was getting a wedgie. Not just an ordinary wedgie. He was getting an atomic wedgie. A bruno named Malone was yanking the poor sap's underwear up to his armpits. Gregory glanced in the direction of the bushes I was hiding behind. His face was contorted in pain. Malone gave one last yank, and Gregory's tighty-whitey's finally ripped off. Gregory crumpled to the ground, writhing, and Malone did a victory lap around the back lot waving Gregory's underwear in the air like a flag. I pressed the stop button on my camera. I had the whole nasty scene saved on digital, and pretty soon Principal Snit would have it, too. My client was hoping it would get Malone tossed out of Iona High for good. I had my doubts that a wedgie, no matter how heinous, would get anyone kicked out of school for more than a week, but my job wasn't giving advice. I was a P.I., and my job was doing what my clients wanted, no questions asked. I was just starting to stand up when someone jumped behind the bushes I'd been using as cover.

"What's the deal?" I asked, worried this guy might be one of Malone's goons.

"Stay down," he said, grabbing my shoulder and shoving me close to the ground. He was a big guy, but no taller than six foot six, and no more than three hundred pounds. His hand was about the size of my head, and it felt like he might break my shoulder if he didn't let go soon.

"Easy there, boss," I groaned. "I'm not going anywhere."

"Huh?" he said, not looking at me. He was peering over the bush, but I couldn't see what he was looking at.

"Could you ease up on my shoulder, brother? I won't blow your cover. I promise."

He was wearing a black jacket with the hood up and a ball cap pulled low underneath, so I couldn't get a good look at his face. "Oh, sorry," he said, releasing his grip. "Just stay down."

"I'll hold tight, but can you tell me what we're supposed to be looking at?"

"Across the field," he said in a whisper. "The can."

"The garbage can?" I asked, following his gaze to the far side of the football field. "The one next to the bleachers?"

"I just made the drop," he whispered. "They'll be here soon."

The two of us squatted there, watching the garbage can, but no one came to pick anything up. The first bell rang, and my oversized friend glanced at his watch. Four or five kids who were finishing their cigarettes flicked butts on the ground and filed into the school.

"They've got to come. They've got to," he whispered again. We both sat and watched the can in silence. The back lot was completely empty.

"What's in the can?" I asked. He didn't answer.

I was supposed to be slipping the disk of Gregory's assault under Snit's door. I was supposed to be in chemistry class. I was supposed to be minding my own business. So, of course, I stuck around. "Hey! Wise guy!" I said, trying to get his attention. "What's in the can?"

"Shh! Be quiet!" he whispered.

"I'll be quiet when you let me know what's in the garbage can, friend."

"Would you be quiet!" he hissed. "Who are you, anyway?" he asked, finally turning to face me.

"Easy, guy, you're the one who invited me to stay for this party, remember? I'm just wondering what the surprise is going to be."

He glared at me for a second, then glanced at his watch again. "Why aren't they coming to get it?"

I was beginning to think this guy was loony tunes, and I didn't like the idea of spending my morning hiding in the bushes with a goofy galoot. "Look, pal, I don't know what game you're playing at, but if you don't bring me into the loop PDQ, then I'm getting up and going inside."

"It's an essay, all right?" he said. "Now be quiet."

"Why did you put an essay in a garbage can?"

"I put it in the can because someone's got Carver. That's why. Because they have Carver," he said, punching the ground with one giant fist.

"Who's Carver?"

"Here," he said, pulling a folded piece of paper out of his jacket and tossing it to me. It was a picture of a hamster standing in front of a newspaper. There was a message scrawled in red letters across the bottom: "Write the essay, or the rodent dies."

"Carver's a hamster," I said.

He turned to me seriously. "Yeah, Carver's a hamster. He's my hamster."

"So, whoever has Carver made you write this essay for them, or Carver gets to meet his maker?"

"That's right," he said, turning to me. "Say, you put that together pretty quick. Are you in on this?"

He looked suspicious, and I didn't like the idea of a guy that big (and possibly nutso) getting suspicious. "I don't know thing one about your essay, and I definitely don't know anything about Carver the hamster. I do know a little something about blackmail. I know too much about it. See, I solve problems, and blackmail seems to be a problem that's going around Iona High in spades."

"You solve problems? What are you, like a detective or something?"

"Detective, private eye, gumshoe, last resort — you can call me whatever you like."

"Well," he said, staring over the bush, "I wish you could solve this problem."

"That can be arranged," I said.

"How's that?"

"Like I said, I solve problems for people. I could solve this one for you. But before you put me on the case, you should know there's a price. There's always a price."

"Oh yeah," he said, narrowing his eyes. "What's that?"

"If I solve this problem for you, then sometime down the line, I'll pay you a visit, and I'll need a favor. That's the price; nothing too outrageous, just a small favor." I held up my hands to show him this wasn't a con job.

"Man, if you can find Carver, you can ask me for whatever you want."

"Then it looks like I'm on the case," I said, holding out my hand. "Name's Jack Lime."

"Tyrone Jonson," he said, shaking my hand. I was afraid he might break it. The late bell rang, and he checked his watch again. "I'm going to be late for pre-cal."

"That's why you hire a peeper like me, Tyrone. So you can drift off to class and I'll make sure nobody walks away with your essay."

"All right," he said, getting up and heading for the door. He stopped halfway, turned around and came back. "What were you doing hiding in the bushes in the first place?"

"I solve problems, Tyrone. Sometimes that means hiding behind bushes."

He looked at me sideways, sizing me up. "If that essay's gone, I'm going to come looking for you."

"That's fair," I said, and he turned to go. "Hey, Tyrone," I called, and I was about to ask him if he'd slip Gregory's disk under Snit's door. Then I remembered Rule One for any detective worth his salt: don't trust anyone. That's a lesson I learned the hard way, thanks to a dame named Jennifer O'Rourke. Her case involved a trivia contest, a fake bookcase and a few incriminating photos, but that's another story.

"What do you want?" he asked while I reconsidered.

"After first period, could you bring me a root beer?" I said, trying to cover up.

"Does that count as the favor?"

"No," I said. "But it's fixing to be a scorcher, and I don't want to melt in this heat."

Monday, June 2, 2:02 p.m.
Iona High, The Back Lot

I'd just spent an entire day staking out a garbage can instead of going to classes. Normally, that would make me edgy, but I was too hot to be edgy. Good thing Tyrone was bringing me my fourth bottle of water that day. (Selling soda in school had been nixed by the powers that be, so root beer was out of the question.) I thought the jacket he'd been wearing when I first met him might have bulked him up, but he wasn't wearing his jacket this time, and he was just as big as I remembered. He'd be easy to find in a hurry. Besides being a giant, he sported dreadlocks that shot out from his head like a water fountain, and he wore thick, black-rimmed glasses. I had to wonder why I'd never noticed him before. Maybe I was slipping.

"Bad news," I said, as he squatted down beside me. "No one's even glanced at that can all day. Not even a whiff of interest."

"I can't figure it out," he said, already sweating a little. "Why would someone make me write an essay and then not come to pick it up?"

"Maybe they're patient," I said.

"What d'you mean?"

"They might be back after school or maybe even tonight. But I have to level with you, Tyrone; I can't stick around here forever. I'll stay until five, then I have to head home. When my grandmother finds out I cut classes today, I'll fry, but if I'm late for supper, she'll have the fuzz scouring the town for me again. That will mean a month under glass, and then I won't be any good to you. Tomorrow we'll try this thing from a different angle, but it's too hot for all this chitchat right now. Here's my card," I said, pulling out my wallet. I passed a card to Tyrone. "My number's on it. Meet me in the cafeteria tomorrow morning at eight. Call if you can't make it."

Tyrone stuffed the card into his pants pocket and headed back inside as the bell rang for last period. I hunkered down with my water and prayed for the kind of action that would make a day in this heat worthwhile.

Tuesday, June 3, 8:09 a.m.
Iona High, The Cafeteria

I was sitting at the back of the cafeteria, eating a bacon and egg sandwich and sipping on a frosty root beer that I had picked up on the way to school when Tyrone blew in through the main doors.

"Did they pick it up?" he asked as soon as he reached me.

"Nope," I said. "I stuck around until five, but the place was a ghost town. By then, even the teachers had gone home."

"I don't understand it," he said, sitting down next to me. "I just don't understand it."

"Tyrone, if I'm going to help you, I'm going to need some info. Why don't you tell me how this crazy dance got started. From the beginning this time."

"Well, a little over two months ago, I brought Carver to school for a biology experiment. I was working from the hypothesis that small mammals could relate previous learned experiences to —"

"Whoa, whoa, whoa there, Chatty Cathy," I said, cutting him off. "I don't need to know about the experiment. Just give me the facts."

"But the experiment proved that —"

"Just the facts," I repeated.

"All right, but you're missing out on a fascinating case study. So let's see, where was I? Right. After I finished my presentation, the lunch bell rang. I left Carver in his cage in the lab for lunch, and when I got back, he was gone. If I'd just left the camera running, I'd know who had him."

"You were recording your lab?"

"I always record my projects. That way, I can watch them again and see if I made any mistakes, or if there were any variables I didn't consider. Science is all about observation, you know."

Tyrone didn't fit the part, but there was no doubt about it; I was working for the biggest pinhead in the school. And when I say biggest, I mean that in every possible way. This guy could probably carry all the other pinheads around on his back.

"I know all about observation, Tyrone. Except in my line of work, it usually involves underwear getting ripped off or a pair of muddy shoes instead of hamsters running around in mazes. Tell me what happened after Carver disappeared."

"A couple days later, there was an envelope taped to my locker. Inside was a picture of Carver. There was a message on the back that said to do the French take-home test that was in the envelope or I'd never see Carver again. They told me to put the test in a black garbage bag and drop it in the trash can on the far side of the football field first thing Monday morning."

"The drop's always on Monday mornings?"

Tyrone nodded.

"How many projects have you done?"

"About one a week. I just don't know why they wouldn't pick the stuff up. The extra work is starting to kill me, and then they don't pick the stuff up! It's crazy!"

"They might have," I said, trying to calm him down. "They might have come in the middle of the night, for all we know. We'll check the can as soon as I finish eating, but there's got to be a better way of catching this guy than sitting outside and melting in this heat. I'll need a description of every project you've had to do," I said. "Maybe I can narrow down which classes this fakeloo artist takes based on the assignments you've had to do."

"I can tell you one thing," Tyrone said. "Whoever it is, they're not in any of my classes."

"How's that?" I asked.

"Besides the English essays and the French test, they've given me some economics assignments and an ancient history project."

"What do you take?"

"Physics, pre-cal, advanced chemistry and advanced biology. There's a small group of people who take those classes, and we pretty much follow each other around all day. Plus, the first thing I did was ask around the class. Nobody takes any of those courses this semester."

"That could be important," I said. "Write up that list for me, and I'll start pounding the pavement, knocking on doors and asking the kind of tough questions people don't like to answer."

"No problem," Tyrone said. "Now, let's go check that can."

I didn't argue with him.

Tuesday, June 3, 8:33 a.m.
Iona High, Mr. Kurtz's class

The essay was still in the garbage, right where he'd left it. I told him I couldn't afford missing school two days in a row, so I took his list of projects and headed to my morning class. I had English first, and the essay in the can was on *The Old Man and the Sea*, so I decided to hit up Kurtz with a few razor-sharp questions.

"It's not one of mine," Kurtz said, as students filed into the room. "And I can tell you this, Mr. Lime, it doesn't belong to any other teacher at Iona High."

"What do you mean?" I asked.

"That essay hasn't been assigned in two years. So if your friend is planning on selling it or something, he may as well forget it. It's worthless. Did he find it in the trash?"

"I can't tell you that," I said. "It's confidential."

"First of all," he said, leaning forward in his chair and opening a big binder, "nothing is confidential when it comes to academic fraud. I'll be making a note regarding this conversation and bringing it to the attention of administration. Second, your friend may as well throw that essay out. We don't even have *The Old Man and the Sea* in the book room anymore."

"I don't follow," I said.

"That essay was one of Brian Murdock's assignments. Brian retired two years ago, and we cleared out all the copies of *The Old Man and the Sea* when he left. We needed to make room for some new books. Be thankful for that, Mr. Lime."

"So there's not a single, solitary teacher in this building who would assign this essay?"

"That's right," Kurtz said.

"Why would someone want an essay that's not worth anything?" I mumbled.

"Bad practical joke?" Kurtz said.

Or a mean one, I thought. That's when I had an idea. "Got to go," I said, and bolted out of the room.

"Get back here, Mr. Lime!" Kurtz yelled. "You'll be late! I'll mark you absent!"

The late bell rang just as I stepped out of the school. I raced across the field and tossed the lid off the can. It was empty, completely empty. Even the few cups and soggy cigarette butts that had been sitting at the bottom were gone. Someone had collected the garbage. I raced to the far side of the building where the big green dumpsters sat. Tony Leoni, the school's custodian, was tossing bags into the dumpsters.

"Stop!" I hollered, as I bolted across the field. "Stop!"

"What? What? What do you want, kid?"

"I need to look through those bags!"

"Are you crazy?"

"I dropped something in one of them, and I need to get it back. It's valuable. I need to look through the bags. Please."

"What's with you kids? Last week some mooyuk chucked his wallet in the garbage. He ripped the bag apart, and I had to clean up the mess. So you listen close, kid," he started, leaning in on me. Leoni was short, sported a cheesy handlebar mustache and a comb-over that only covered part of his head. But he had Popeye forearms and a way of walking that made kids step aside in the hallways. "You want to dig through the trash, be my guest, but I'm warning you, if I see one bit of garbage floating around out here when you're done, I'm going to come after you, and when I find you, I'm going to skin you alive. You got that?"

"It'll be spic and span," I promised, crossing my heart. He started to leave, but I had one more question.

"Do you always collect the garbage on Tuesdays?" I said to his back.

He whirled around and leaned into me again, breathing stale coffee into my face. "You know darn well I collect on Mondays, don't you, kid?" he hissed, poking me in the chest with a thick, pudgy finger. "Are you some kind of snitch or something? Did the principal put you up to this? Does Snit want a piece of me?" I thought Leoni might skin me alive right there. "Well you can tell Snit that I had an appointment yesterday. I don't need a snotty kid telling me I'm a day late! I know I'm late!"

"Just wondering," I said, holding up my hands. "Just wondering is all."

Leoni glared at me, then turned and trudged back into the school. "Not one scrap!" he hollered before disappearing into the school.

Folks, there are parts of this P.I. game that are nastier than cleaning the boys' bathroom with a broken toothbrush. Digging around in those dumpsters was one of them. Let's just say that when Principal Snit came out to find me, I was knee deep in filth, covered in sweat and I reeked like the fish burgers we had for lunch a week ago. But I had the essay.

Tuesday, June 3, 9:32 a.m.
A street with no name, Grandma's House

Snit decided I couldn't go back to class stinking like week-old fish burgers, so he wrapped me in some old blankets and drove me home. Apparently, Snit had issues with me skipping classes to work on my investigations. My grandma seemed to have issues with that, too. So we all sat down and had a very pleasant chat over tea and crumpets to address the matter. I made nice with Snit, and they decided that a suspension was out of order, but I had to promise to keep my nose clean. Snit said his good-byes, and I hopped in the shower.

I'll spare you the intimate details of the conversation I had with my grandma after Snit left (if being yelled at counts as a conversation), but let's just say I was in serious trouble. Surprisingly, she wasn't excited about me finding Tyrone's essay, and she wasn't interested in listening to reason. But I could understand where she was coming from. Grandma had been enjoying her golden years when little old me arrived on the scene, looking for trouble. I apologized and promised to stay on the straight and narrow. Then I kissed my grandma good-bye and headed back to Iona High. I needed to see Tyrone, and fast.

Tuesday, June 3, 12:31 p.m.
Iona High, The Cafeteria

Tyrone was about as hard to find in the cafeteria as a wolf at a sheep convention. Except in this case, he was the sheep, and somewhere in the crowd there was a wolf who was ready to bite the head off little old Carver if I didn't watch my step. Tyrone was sitting at the back with two empty trays of food in front of him and a physics textbook jammed under his nose. I tossed the essay onto the table.

He grimaced at the stink before he realized what it was. "What are you doing!" he cried. "If that's not in the can, Carver's a goner!"

"Relax," I said, sitting down. "I haven't figured it all

out yet, but I think we're dealing with a fakeloo artist who's just blowing a lot of hot air."

"What are you talking about?"

"I talked to my English teacher today. We don't even have a copy of *The Old Man and the Sea* at Iona High. The teacher who used to torture his students with this particular essay retired two years ago. Plus, Leoni collects the garbage on Mondays. I don't think your hamster-napper ever intended on making off with this essay or any of your work. It all just got collected with the trash."

"I don't understand," he said and pounded the table with his hands. The two trays jumped six inches and landed with a crash. The cafeteria got quiet, and quick. I think they were expecting Tyrone to rip my head off.

"Nothing to see here," I said, turning to face the room full of slack-jawed gawkers. "There's nothing to see here, kids." For the time being, everyone went back to their business.

"Why would someone get me to write an essay that was never assigned and that they'd never pick up?" Tyrone hissed.

"That's why I'm here. I need to pick your brain. Who would get a kick out of you doing a whole bunch of projects? Why would someone do that to you?"

"Well," Tyrone started, "it's kept me pretty busy. I mean, it's kept me up late, and I don't have much time for my own homework. It's made my grades slip a little."

"That's a start," I said. "What kind of grades do you get?"

"Perfect grades."

"What do you mean, perfect?"

"Perfect. One hundred percent."

"You always get one hundred percent? On everything?"

"I used to, until Carver disappeared. The extra work has hurt me. I think I've got a ninety-eight average now."

"A ninety-eight average? And you take pre-cal, physics, chemistry and biology?"

"Advanced chemistry and biology. Unfortunately, there's no advanced physics here."

"Jeesh, I guess I thought those kinds of grades were reserved for fairy tales."

"No fairy tale," Tyrone said. "I need those grades so I can win the Luxemcorp Prize. If I don't win that, I'm not going to university."

FYI — When Luxemcorp was done creating this little slice of suburban heaven called Iona, they needed to convince city slickers to move into their gated metropolis. So they threw in the kinds of perks that only a gazillion-dollar multinational conglomerate is able to offer; things like free Segways, golf course memberships, a high-speed train to zip them into the city, a sprinkling of classy boutiques and a smattering of hip restaurants. Plus, one gigantic scholarship for the top high school graduate. In honor of themselves, they called it the Luxemcorp Prize.

"How much is that worth?" I asked.

"Thirty-five grand each year you're in university," he said, and then slammed his hand down on the table, sending the trays flying again. "That's it!" he yelled. "They're after the scholarship! They want me to lose!" The cafeteria was dead quiet again. All eyes were on us.

"Tyrone," I said, "why don't we walk and talk." We'd already drawn too much attention to ourselves. "If the person who has Carver knows we're on to him," I whispered on our way out, "Carver's life might be in danger."

"I can't believe I didn't figure this out earlier!" Tyrone said once we were in the hall. He hit his forehead with an open hand. If he'd hit me like that, my head would have cracked open like an egg. "It's got to be someone going after the scholarship."

"There can't be too many on that list," I said. "Do you have anyone in mind?"

"I don't know ... not really. I mean, I thought they were my friends."

"There's got to be someone who's close to your grades who might want to take you out of the running."

"I never thought about someone doing that."

"Think," I said. "Who's your main competition?"

"Well, there are only two people who are really close to me," he said. "Walter Hampton and Polly Chew; they've both got averages in the high nineties."

"Then we just have to track them down and figure out if one of them has Carver. It's a start."

"How are we going to do that?" Tyrone asked. "Like you said, if they know we're on to them, they might kill Carver."

"Do you have that picture of Carver they sent you?"

He pulled it out of his pocket and handed it to me. I scanned the photo, looking for some kind of clue. Then it hit me. It was right in front of us, in black and white.

"Look at the paper," I said.

"What?" he asked. "What am I looking for?"

"The bum who's pulling this con job takes these snapshots of Carver so you know he's alive the day he took the picture. The date's right there, at the top of the page. But there's something else at the top of the page," I said, pointing at the paper.

"*The Daily Telegraph*," he said.

"That's right," I said. "We just need to stake out Hampton and Chew and find out which one gets *The Daily Telegraph*."

"You're brilliant," Tyrone said, patting me on the back so hard I thought he might have knocked a tooth loose.

"I'll take Hampton. You take Chew," I said. "I figure the paper will get there around seven, so we should be in place by six-thirty, just to be on the safe side."

"There's a bit of a problem with that plan, Jack," Tyrone said.

"What?"

"I don't get here until eight in the morning."

"What do you mean, 'get here'?"

"I don't live here," he said. "I live in the city. My dad works at Sam the Butcher's on Main. We come in on the train every morning at eight."

"Huh? Really? I guess I thought everyone who went to Iona High lived here."

"Nope," he said, shaking his head. "There are a few of us who come in from the city. My dad heard about the Luxemcorp Prize at work, so he took me out of my school in the city and registered me for classes here so

I'd have a shot at winning the scholarship."

"That's why I've never seen you around before."

"This is my first year here."

"And that's probably why you've got someone upset enough that they're willing to kill Carver. They probably figured they had the scholarship wrapped up until Mr. Perfect-Grades-from-the-City showed up and spoiled their plans."

"Probably," he said, nodding.

"Now things are starting to make sense. Look, I've got some favors I can call in. I'll line up someone to stake out Chew, and I'll watch Hampton. I'll let you know how it turns out tomorrow morning."

"Thanks, Jack," Tyrone said, and we went our separate ways.

Wednesday, June 4, 7:02 a.m.
34 Kuiper Belt Crescent, The Hampton Place

There I was, squatting behind the neighbor's fence, waiting for the Hamptons to get their paper. This line of work isn't all glitz and glamor, that's for sure. Ninety-nine percent of the time, it's dreary, dirty and dull. It's about rooting around in dumpsters and eating a stale granola bar you found in your pocket for breakfast instead of your grandma's buttermilk pancakes because you're waiting for the morning paper to show up, and the kicker is, you're not going to get to read it. But when the action happens, all that waiting pays off — big time. The newsie had just turned the corner on his bike, tossing papers onto lawns as he went, and he was heading my way.

I hunkered down and waited for him to pass by, then I scurried across the street to see what the Hamptons liked to read with their morning coffee. Bingo! It was *The Daily Telegraph*. I was just about to drop the paper back onto their step when the front door flew open, and two people rushed out.

"Thanks, kid," the first one said, grabbing the paper out of my hand. He was tall, thin as a rail, with wispy gray hair that poked out from under a black fedora, and had a nose that was as long and sharp as a hatchet. I figured that was Mr. Hampton. "Hurry up," he said. "We're going to be late for the train again." Behind him, pulling on a long black trench coat, was a younger man with the same build and the same hatchet nose, but he had black hair instead of gray.

"I forgot my bag," the younger one said. He turned, started back, tripped on the top step and practically fell into the house.

"Good grief," the older Hampton said, getting into the car. The younger one came back out and dashed by me. This time, he missed the bottom step, tripped across the front walk and did a face plant on the lawn. The older Hampton couldn't help but laugh. He was still laughing when they backed out of the driveway.

I turned back to the house, having a little chuckle of my own. A kid who looked just like the first two Hamptons, but with blond hair, was standing in the door, staring out at me. I smiled and nodded, not wanting to blow my cover. He slammed the door shut. That must have been Walter. I started back to the street and pulled out the walkie-talkie I had in my jacket.

"Any luck, Max?" I asked. Max Thorn was on the other end at Polly Chew's house. I was running low on favors, so Max was the only person I could round up on short notice for early morning surveillance work. I could picture him hanging from a tree branch with a set of binoculars taped to his head. Max might be goofy, but he gets the job done, and he knows how to keep his mouth shut if I tell him it's confidential.

"They get *The Telegraph*, Chief," he said. "Over."

"*The Daily Telegraph*?" I asked.

"Roger that, Chief," he said. "What's our next move? Over."

"Go home," I said. "The stakeout's a bust."

"Shouldn't we stick around in case there's some kind of cover-up?" he asked. "Over."

"Cover-up?" I said. "Max, you're nuttier then a carload of squirrels. Go home, and that's an order."

"Roger Wilco, Chief. I'll have my report on your desk by 0-nine hundred hours. Thorn out."

Thorn Out, Lime Out, the whole rotten case was out. This job was turning into a real brain twister, and I was getting nowhere fast.

Wednesday, June 4, 8:17 a.m.
Iona High, The Science Hallway

Things were getting desperate for yours truly. I hate to admit it, but on my way back to school, I started to wonder if Carver was worth it. Thirty-five grand could buy a lot of hamsters, even after all the other expenses of getting a high-class education. I found Tyrone standing alone in the science hallway, staring at pictures of the illustrious winners of Iona High's Science Fair, past and present.

"Is your handsome mug going to be hanging up there soon?" I asked, trying to sound positive.

"Did you find out who it is? Is it Polly?" he said, ignoring me.

I shook my head. "We struck out. They both get *The Daily Telegraph*."

"Oh," he said, turning back to the pictures. "I don't know. Maybe it's not worth it."

"I was thinking the same thing," I said, feeling relieved. "After all, you can get another hamster."

Tyrone whirled around, grabbed me by my collar and lifted me off the ground. "My mother gave me that hamster three years ago. She died two weeks later. Do you have any idea how hard it is to keep a hamster alive for three years? *Do you*?"

To be honest, at that moment, I didn't really care how hard it was to keep a hamster alive for three years. I was more concerned with keeping myself out of a coffin for three more seconds.

"It was a stupid suggestion," I said.

"It was," Tyrone said, and then he lowered me back to the ground. "It was a very stupid suggestion. I was talking about the scholarship, not Carver. So what are we going to do now?"

I didn't know what I was going to do now. Chew and Hampton were just two possible suspects. It could have been anyone who was interested in winning the Luxemcorp Prize. Or it could have been anyone who didn't want Tyrone to win the prize. I was getting nowhere fast.

"I guess I can see why they'd be mad at me," he mumbled, more to the wall of pictures than to me.

I followed his gaze. All the people in the pictures were smiling back at us without a care in the world. There was Amelia Freeman dressed in a white lab coat and holding a beaker full of blue stuff. Next to her was Glenn Paterson standing beside a bubbling barrel of red goo. Then there was David Philips holding a blowtorch and laughing, and next to him was Ralph Hampton squirting some kind of liquid out of a syringe. Wait a minute. There was Ralph Hampton squirting some kind of liquid out of a syringe. Ralph Hampton; the same Ralph Hampton I watched fall on his face that morning. There was no doubt about that sharp honker of his. You could slice tomatoes on that thing. Under his picture was a small gold engraving that read: *First Prize — Grade 12 Science Fair — Awarded to Ralph Hampton*. So Ralphy had graduated from Iona High two years ago. Fireworks went off in my head. Connections were being made. Things were starting to make sense.

"I have to go," I said, yanking the picture off the wall.

Wednesday, June 4, 8:26 a.m.
Iona High, The Guidance Office

Ms. Mickle knew everyone who had passed through Iona High's front doors since it had opened twelve years ago. She was wearing a long, puffy yellow skirt, a red sweater and two giant orange hoop earrings. Her curly gray hair was going in eight directions at once.

"Ms. Mickle," I said, holding up the picture, "do you know this guy?"

"Well if it isn't Jack Lime. Come in, come in," she said, tapping a chair next to her. "You haven't been in recently. You know that Dr. Potter recommended you see me every week."

"Been busy," I said. "And I'm in a bit of a rush. I just wanted to know if you knew Ralph Hampton."

"I heard you had some problems yesterday with an assignment you lost in the garbage?" she said, looking concerned.

"I found what I was looking for," I said. "Please, Ms. Mickle, do you know Ralph Hampton?"

"Ralph Hampton?" she said, as if it was the first time I'd mentioned him. "Now, that name sounds familiar."

The first bell rang, and I gave up trying to be quick about this. I walked into her office, sat down and handed her the picture. "Ralph Hampton," I repeated, tapping on the photo.

She leaned back and closed her eyes for a long time. For a second, I thought she'd fallen asleep, and then she blurted, "Oh, sure, Ralph Hampton. He was smart as a whip, but the clumsiest kid I ever met. Do you know he set himself on fire in his economics class? He didn't even have any matches."

"In economics class," I asked, to make sure I was hearing her right.

"Yes, it was the strangest thing I'd ever seen. But, oh my, he was a smarty-pants. He was our top student until Cindy Hooper came here."

"Cindy Hooper?"

"Cindy came here her senior year. Her parents moved from Boston. I think her father was a professor ... or a scientist ... or maybe an engineer. No, I think he was a lawyer. Oh, I guess it doesn't matter now, does it? Anyway, Cindy was only fifteen, but she was the brightest young lady we've ever had at our school. She was a genius. A real genius! Poor Ralph probably would have won the Luxemcorp Prize if she hadn't arrived on our doorstep. Poor Ralph."

"Thanks, Ms. Mickle," I said, getting up.

"Don't forget a lolli on your way out, Jack," she said, pointing to a bowl full of lollipops next to her door.

As I was going out, Gregory "Atomic Wedgie" Pepperton was on his way in.

"Jack," he said, grabbing me by the shoulders. "Malone only got five days. He'll be back in five days, and he says he's coming after me. You have to help. You have to!"

Gregory was looking pretty rotten. He was as white as a sheet and sweating like a hog.

"Get in touch," I said, struggling out of his grip. "Call me." I tossed three or four of my cards over my shoulder.

I felt awful about Gregory. I really did. But I needed to focus on helping Tyrone, and the pieces of the puzzle were coming together.

Here's what I knew so far:

1. Ralph Hampton had taken economics. (Apparently, he'd almost set himself on fire.)
2. Tyrone had been given an economics project to finish.
3. Ralph had graduated two years ago, which meant he could have had Murdock for his English teacher, and he probably would have done the essay on *The Old Man and the Sea*.
4. Tyrone was given that exact same essay to finish two years after the novel had been cleared out of the book room.
5. Ralph had lost the most prestigious scholarship to a girl who arrived on the scene at the last minute.
6. Tyrone had arrived at Iona High at the last minute, and now he was about to steal the Luxemcorp Prize out from under Walter Hampton's sharp nose.

Tyrone was moving in on sacred territory, and the blond model of the Hampton family wasn't going to let anything stand in his way of winning the Luxemcorp Prize. He'd gotten his slimy little fingers on some of his brother's old work, and now he was making Tyrone do useless projects to keep him so busy that he'd lose the scholarship. Well, I was tired of squatting in bushes, holding early morning stakeouts and rooting around in dumpsters. It was time to take the bull by the horns, to stand and deliver, to draw a line in the sand. I was going to pay Walter Hampton a little visit, and I was going to get Carver back. Things might get rough; they might even get a little messy, but I was okay with rough and messy as long as I could shut the lid on this dirty case.

Wednesday, June 4, 3:43 p.m.
34 Kuiper Belt Crescent, The Hampton Place

I avoided Tyrone like the plague for the rest of the day. I was tired of talk. The next time I saw him, I wanted to have Carver in hand. I was out of school before the bell finished ringing and made a dash for the Hampton place. I was sitting on his steps when Walter stepped onto his front walk.

"Hello, Walter," I said, getting up. "I think we both know why I'm here."

"Who are you?" he asked, stopping in his tracks.

"You want to play it that way?" I said. "That's fine. Let's play it coy. My name's Jack Lime. You probably know my client, Tyrone Jonson."

"Sure, I know Tyrone," he said, playing the innocent rube.

"Still playing it dumb? Well, I'm tired of that game, Walter. I'm really tired of it. So why don't we cut to the chase." I marched over to him. We were face to face. "You've got something that Tyrone wants back, and I'm here to collect it."

"I don't know what you're talking about."

"Something small and furry," I said. "You like to get it to pose for dirty pictures. Ringing any bells?"

"Get out of my way," he said, and tried to push past me. I grabbed him and spun him around to face me again.

"No dice," I said. "You're not going anywhere until you fess up to the kidnapping and the blackmail scam you've been playing at. It's a filthy graft, Hampton, and as sure as ten dimes make a dollar you're the one pulling the strings."

That's when Walter did some fancy judo moves that sent me back, then up, and then down to the ground. Before I knew what had hit me, he had his knee pressed into my back, and I was sucking face with the grass.

"Now you listen to me, clown," he said. "Yeah, I've got the rodent. He's upstairs, in my room, probably asleep in an old toilet paper tube. It doesn't matter if you know, or if Tyrone knows. Actually, this will make things much easier. You can be my messenger boy. Go tell Tyrone if he wants to see Carver alive, he'd better get me some research on the wind turbine project we've got for physics class. Tell him I want it by Friday, and it'd better be good."

"Why would he do that?" I gasped, trying to get myself out of Walter's wrestling hold.

"Because if he doesn't, I'm going to feed Carver to my pet python, Cindy. How's that sound?"

"How does he know you'll give him Carver back?"

"He'll get Carver back the day I leave for university next fall. And he'd better make sure that I'm going with a thirty-five-thousand-dollar check in my pocket. You got that?"

I could feel him ease up on my back, so I shifted my weight quickly to my right. He slipped off, and I was about to pounce on him like a cat on a mouse. Unfortunately, that's when my condition kicked in.

I dreamed I was getting squeezed by a python. Two hamsters were up in a tree staring down at me. They were holding a sword in their tiny little hands. One of them wanted to drop it on me. The other one said they should wait. The python squeezed a little tighter. "Drop it!" the first hamster yelled in a high-pitched voice. "Wait!" the other one screamed. They struggled, and the sword slipped out of their hands. It fell toward me. Then I woke up.

Wednesday, June 4, 4:47 p.m.
41 Main Street, Sam the Butcher's

There is no Sam at Sam the Butcher's. There never was a Sam. The place is owned and operated by Luxemcorp Inc., the same company that owns all the stores in Iona (except The Diner). Luxemcorp just slaps hokey names on each store so people think they're quaint, family-owned businesses. It was supposed to make everyone feel warm and fuzzy. Tyrone was sitting in the corner of the place reading a chemistry textbook. When I walked in, he jumped up.

"Jack! Am I glad to see you. I worked out the problem."

"I've got some news, too," I said.

"Whoever's getting me to do this," he started, ignoring me, "thinks that I don't know about the whole garbage collection thing. They think that I think they're actually handing the stuff in. But I know they don't even look at it. So, all I have to do is put some paper in a black garbage bag and make the drop every Monday, and they'll never know the difference. That way, I can focus on my work and still win the Luxemcorp Prize."

"Great," I said, "but —"

"No, no, wait, it gets better. Whoever has Carver can't kill him, or I'll stop doing the extra work. They want Carver to stay alive. As long as he's alive, I'll have to do the assignments for them. It's called leverage. So Carver will be safe until we figure out a way to save him. I worked it all out in physics class. It hit me like a meteor dropping on my head. It's all so obvious that I can't believe I didn't think about it sooner."

"Yeah," I said. "I wish you had figured that out sooner."

"What do you mean?"

"I paid a visit to Ms. Mickle, the guidance counselor, today. She told me some things about Ralph Hampton that made me think that Walter was our man. So I decided to pay him a visit after school."

"And?"

"He's got Carver."

I watched Tyrone's beefy fists clench shut.

"And he doesn't care if you know it. Like you said, he's got leverage."

"What's he going to do?"

"Nothing," I said. I decided to serve Tyrone the sitch straight up. "He's going to keep Carver alive, and he's going to keep you working overtime. Only now you'll be doing real work instead of stuff that winds up in the trash."

"So," he said, his eyes narrowing, "you've made things worse."

"I've made things a whole lot worse, Tyrone," I said. "And I've got a message." I pulled one of my business cards out of my pocket. Walter must have grabbed it when I was asleep and written a message on the back so I wouldn't forget. "Walter wants you to do some research on some wind turbine project you have for physics. And he wants it by Friday." I held out the card. Tyrone snatched it out of my hand.

"Well," Tyrone said, his massive shoulders slumping as he sat back down, "at least I've got most of that done already."

"You're a keener," I said, "through and through."

"Not really," he said. The anger had gone right out of him. "I did something just like this for my Science Fair project last year. I just have to find the copy of the video."

"You've got a video of your Science Fair project?"

"Of course," he said. "I record all of my projects, remember?"

An idea hit me like a runaway locomotive. "Tyrone," I said, "I know I've botched things pretty bad, but I think I know a way to make everything right again."

"I don't know, Jack," he said, shaking his massive head. "I think it's time to go our separate ways."

"Just hear me out. I need you to go home and write a paper on wind turbines that's so good Walter Hampton will think three times before he decides not to use it. Just make sure you use the exact same words you used in the original video; use the same terms, the same phrases. Make sure anyone who reads that paper will know that it's based on your first project. You see where I'm going with this?"

He brightened a little. "It might work," he said. "It's worth a try."

"Then *we'll* have some leverage, for once," I said.

Monday, June 9, 3:43 p.m.
34 Kuiper Belt Crescent, The Hampton Place

It was the last Monday of classes before exams started. All the wind turbine projects had been handed in. Grade 12 physics students all over Iona High were celebrating. I was sitting on the front steps at the Hampton residence waiting for Walter to get back home.

"Hello, Walter," I said, as he stepped onto his front walk. "Good to see you again."

"What do you want, Lime? Another beating?"

"How did the wind turbine project go?"

"Fine," he said, stepping up to me. "Just fine."

"All handed in and wrapped with a bow?"

"That's right," he said. "Now, could you get out of my way? I have a hamster to feed. And a python, too."

"You don't have to worry about Carver anymore," I said.

"What are you blabbering about now?"

I pulled a DVD out of my pocket. "You know what's on this? A video of the winning Science Fair project from

City Heights High School. It's all about wind turbines. Tyrone Jonson did it last year. It's fantastic. You should watch it, Wally."

Walter pursed his lips, and his nose got a little sharper. He snatched the DVD out of my hand.

"You're welcome, Wally. Consider it a graduation present. Of course, there are plenty of copies: one for your physics teacher, one for Principal Snit, one for the execs at Luxemcorp. They might get a special delivery this week. But that depends on whether or not you give up Carver."

"There's nothing on this," Walter spat at me.

"There's lots of good material on there, Walter. You can watch it to your heart's content tonight. And you'd better hope your paper isn't too much like Tyrone's Science Fair project. Think back, Wally: how much did you use out of the paper Tyrone sent you? A little? A lot? Academic fraud would take you out of the running for the Luxemcorp Prize PDQ."

"I'm going to kill that little ball of fur right now," he barked, stepping by me. "I'll feed it to Cindy!"

"That's a lose-lose situation, Wally," I said, before he got inside. "You'd be out of the running for the big prize, and Tyrone loses his precious hamster. But Tyrone will get over it, I'm sure. Thirty-five grand a year will do that to a person. Plus, he'll finally get the chance to stuff you in a toilet paper roll without worrying about Carver getting fed to a snake. I don't think you'd look good stuffed in a toilet paper roll, Wally. How about you? No, I think the smarter play would be you bringing Carver down here now and taking your chances on the prize the right way, the fair way, using your brain instead of Tyrone's."

"How do I know you won't send the disks anyway?"

"It's called leverage, Wally. We send the DVDs, and we lose our leverage. You should know that."

Monday, June 9, 5:28 p.m.
2 Main Street, The Train Station

The train station is a busy place at rush hour. Parents are getting home from a hard day's work. Kids are crowding onto the trains to go earn a dime at part-time jobs in the city. But Tyrone Jonson is not a hard person to find, even in a crowd.

"Thanks again, Jack," he said, putting Carver into his cage and draping a blanket over it.

"I'm just glad you've got him back."

"How did Walter take it?"

"Not good," I said. "I'd keep an eye on him for the rest of the year."

"I'm not worried," Tyrone said, "as long as we've got some leverage."

"That reminds me," I said. "I've got an atomic wedgie to record tonight."

"What?" Tyrone asked.

"More leverage," I said. "More leverage."

THE CASE OF THE BIG DUPE

Friday, September 27, 5:51 p.m.
Iona Hospital, Room 234

I woke up in a fog as thick as a three-day-old cup of joe. I didn't have a clue where I was or how I got there, so I tried to sit up and have a look around. Problem was, my head felt as if it'd been cracked open like an egg at a Sunday brunch, so the world went topsy-turvy faster than you can say concussion. I flopped back down and tried to suss out my situation, but thanks to all that fog, I couldn't see much except shadows. And the longer I looked, the more shadows there seemed to be. Soon they were all around me, watching me, closing in on me. I was completely surrounded.

"Hay ack," I slurred, throwing my hands in the air, but they just fell back down like two dead fish.

And that's when a voice whispered from the shadows, "Ake ideez hack."

That kind of gobbledygook made me nervous, but hard as I tried, I just couldn't manage to sit up.

"Hake id eez, Jack," the voice said, as one of the shadows broke off from the rest and lurched toward me.

"Hay ack," I slurred, but it kept coming, getting closer and closer.

"Ake it eezy," the voice said. The shadow was standing over me now, like a spider over a fly.

"Ack off!" I yelled, swinging my fists into the darkness.

The shadow leaned over. The darkness covered me like a funeral cloak. I was sure I'd be taking the next train to Deadtown. Then a light flicked on. And in a flash, the shadow was gone and I was face to face with Old Doc Potter.

"Take it easy, Jack," he said, dodging my punches. "You must've been having a dream."

I glanced around the room and realized I was in the hospital — again. "How'd I get here, Doc?" I asked.

"I was hoping you could explain that," Potter said, taking a little flashlight out of his pocket and shining it in my eyes. "All I know is that your principal brought you in after a schoolyard fight, and it looks like you lost. You've been unconscious for almost two hours."

Now that he mentioned it, a nasty brawl did ring a few bells. But all I could remember were four hairy knuckles coming at me like a runaway locomotive. "So what's the damage this time, Doc?"

"A nasty concussion and a broken nose," he said. He sat in a chair next to my bed. "Your grandmother tells me you're still the local crime fighter. Is that true?"

"Say, where is Grandma, anyway?" I asked, touching the bandages on my nose.

"I sent her home to get some rest. But you didn't answer my question: are you still the local crime fighter?"

"Crime fighter, detective, private eye, sleuth, peeper for hire, you can call it a lot of different things. Long story short, I fix problems for people who need problems fixed. Which is a lot like what you do, isn't it, Doc?"

"I suppose you're right about that, Jack," Potter said, leaning back in his seat, "but I don't end up at the hospital as much as you do."

"That's saying something, Doc, considering you're supposed to work here."

"Only part time, Jack," he said. "I'm trying to retire, but I'm worried if I did that you'd end up in the morgue. And I feel like I have a duty to your father to make sure that doesn't happen. Did I ever tell you I was the doctor who delivered your father?"

"I think you've mentioned it once or twice, Doc." In fact, just about every time I saw Doc Potter, he reminded me that he'd delivered my father, which usually led into the you-should-take-better-care-of-yourself lecture, and I could smell that coming a mile away.

"Well, I did, and I would like to think that I'm one of the reasons he became a doctor. You know, he used to come visit me at the hospital just to —"

"Doc, I hate to cut you off, but my head is ready to split open, so why don't we cut to the chase."

"That's fair, Jack. That's fair," he said, stretching out his long legs. "It's time that you started to take better care of yourself, and your poor grandmother, and stopped trying to solve everybody else's problems."

"It's not like I go looking for trouble, Doc. Trouble just has a nasty way of showing up on my doorstep. Heck, I didn't even get into the P.I. business on purpose. It found me."

"How, exactly, does that happen?" he said, sitting forward in his chair.

"I don't know if you want to hear that long and sordid tale, Doc."

"Jack, let me tell you something. Tonight Mrs. Potter plays bridge with the girls. And when Mrs. Potter goes out to play bridge, all I get to go home to is a half-blind dog and a cold dinner. So a good story sounds a lot better than that."

"Suit yourself, Doc, but don't say I didn't warn you."

Potter rolled his eyes.

"I arrived in this little slice of heaven called Iona halfway through Grade 9. It ain't easy making friends in a small town like this, Doc, especially when you're the new kid on the block. For the first couple of months, I might as well have been a ghost to the kids at Iona High. To compensate for being on the bottom of the social pecking order, I threw around enough money to let everyone know I was a big-time player. See, back in the City of Angels, money equaled power, and power equaled popularity. I didn't think Iona would be all that different. So I started spreading around my loot like it was going out of style. I always had the latest and greatest cell phone, I carried a flashy iPod, I had fourteen different pairs of sneakers and I dressed in enough labels to make it look like I just walked out of a magazine.

"FYI — The only reason I could afford all that stuff was

because I got a check in the mail every two weeks that came out of a trust fund set up by the executor of my parents' estate. That's fancy talk for me getting a tidy little bundle of dough every two weeks because my parents died in a car accident, and my Dad's best friend back in L.A., who was in charge of it all, felt guilty about shipping me off to live with my grandmother in a go-nowhere town like Iona.

"But no matter how much cash I threw around, no matter how much I showed off all my cheddar, nothing changed. I kept right on being a big fat nobody. However, there is an upside to being a big fat nobody in a fishbowl like Iona. For one, you get to listen — and you get to watch, and all that listening and watching means you learn a lot of stuff about a lot of people. About a month after my arrival, a girl in my history class figured I might like to do some listening and watching on her behalf.

"The job was simple enough; I just had to watch her boyfriend, a sap named Ryan Morrison, and see if he was a two-timing fink. She offered me twenty bucks a day, and the way I was burning through my dough, I needed all the cash that I could get. As it turns out, Ryan really was a two-timing fink. I took a few snapshots of the dirty dog, she paid me forty bucks and we said our good-byes. That's how I got started in the Private Eye racket."

"You promised me a long and sordid tale, Jack, and that was just short and boring," Potter said, raising one bushy gray eyebrow.

"That's just how I got my start, Doc, but that's not why I'm still in the sleuthing business. It was my second case that kept me in this dirty game. See, since I did such a bang-up job on that case, there were a few people who sat up and took notice of yours truly. One of those people was a girl named Jennifer O'Rourke. She tracked me down in the cafeteria one day, and I haven't been the same since."

Thursday, March 12, 12:17 p.m.
Iona High, The Cafeteria

Jennifer O'Rourke is the kind of girl you want to protect from all the nastiness of the world. She's got silky brown hair that she pulls back in a ponytail, baby-blue eyes and freckles across her nose. She's short and slim and has a way of bouncing when she walks that makes you think everything is going to be all right.

Other than the fact that Jennifer seemed as innocent as a teddy bear at a picnic, I remember our first meeting because I managed to eat a clandestine glob of wasabi that had attached itself onto the back of my sushi. (FYI — Eating sushi for lunch was just one more way I liked to show off my scratch back in those days.) As soon as I swallowed that green glob, it felt like a bundle of dynamite had been set off in my mouth. I actually thought my nose might explode. I was gulping for breath, with tears rolling out of my eyes, when Jennifer strolled over to my table.

"Are you Jack Lime?" she asked. Then she caught a glimpse of my face and started to back away. I might have been a nobody at Iona High, but somehow everyone and their dog knew I was an orphan. So when I looked up and my eyes were rimmed with tears, she must've thought I was getting misty about my parents, when I was actually just trying to survive some extra-hot sushi sauce.

"I'm sorry," she blurted, blushing and averting her eyes. "I'll come back later."

"It's ... all ... right," I croaked. "Please ... sit ..."

"Are you sure? I can come back. I don't —"

"Please," I said, trying to catch my breath. I took a long swig of Red Bull and cleared my throat. "What can I do for you?"

"Well, if you're sure," she said. "A friend of a friend told me you solved a problem for her and that you were very discreet. My colleagues and I require some assistance."

"Your colleagues?"

"Yes," she said, motioning toward a table of three students sitting on the other side of the cafeteria. They were all trying hard not to look at me. "We need some help with a troubling ... situation and would like to hire you in order to rectify this matter."

"Why don't you tell me what kind of situation you need me to rectify, and I'll tell you if I'm your man."

"Tobias Poe is missing."

"Tobias who?"

"Tobias Poe? The top student at Iona High?" she said, like I'd missed the memo. "He's the captain of the chess team and the robotics team, plus he's got the highest GPA in the school. He's the whole reason we're in the Academic All-Stars Trivia Tournament Regional Final on Friday night."

"The Academic what?" I asked.

"The Academic All-Stars Trivia Tournament. And, thanks to Tobias, Iona High has reached the regional finals for the first time ... like, ever."

"And now Tobias is missing?"

"That's right."

"Since when?"

"Since yesterday morning."

"Slow down, sister. I hate to tell you this, but where I come from, when a kid cuts class for a day and a half, it doesn't necessarily mean that he's disappeared."

"He didn't just miss school. Yesterday he missed our team breakfast, our team practice at lunch and our team practice after school. And he isn't here today, either. Plus, he hasn't called any of us."

"Sounds like you spend a lot of time together."

"Yes," she said. "We need to be prepared for our match against Montgomery Academy tomorrow night. If we win that match, we'll progress to the National Championship Tournament. I'm surprised you don't know about it. Everyone in school is going to come and watch. It's even going to be on TV."

"The Regional Final, lots of people watching and it's on TV." I figured that Jennifer and her Merry Band of Geniuses weren't the type of people who craved loads of attention. "Did you ever think that Tobias might just be getting a little nervous and decided to fly the coop?"

"First, Tobias is a very logical person who deals very well with pressure. Second, I called and spoke to his grandfather. He thinks Tobias was at school yesterday. In fact, he told me that Tobias was staying with a friend for the next few days."

"And you didn't blow his cover?" I asked.

"No."

"That's very noble."

"Not really," she said, blushing a little. "If he gets caught skipping classes, he'll be kicked off the team."

"So I have to keep this hush-hush," I said.

"That's right," she said, glancing around the room.

I looked at this girl, so innocent of the ways of the world, and felt sorry for her and her keen-bean friends. My gut was telling me that Tobias was probably just scared out of his britches and didn't want to face the bright lights of a championship game. But I wasn't the kind of guy who turns down a damsel in distress, and I could always use a few more coins jingling in my pockets.

"I get twenty-five bucks a day," I said, jacking up my rate on the fly. I figured a whole team of over-achievers could ante up twenty-five clams without breaking the bank.

"I'll consult with my colleagues," she said, and marched across the cafeteria. They got into a huddle, and I finished my sushi, minus the wasabi.

When they were done deliberating, Jennifer came back to my table. "Twenty-five dollars a day is fine."

"Good," I said, and then threw back the rest of my Red Bull. "Then I need to have a word with the rest of the team."

She motioned them over with a wave, and they all

took a seat around my table. They were a motley crew of oddballs who fit the bill for kids who would excel at a trivia contest.

"I'll need to know a little about each of you, but we need to keep it quick. Just tell me your name, your grade and the last time you saw Tobias, capiche?"

They nodded.

Here's a rundown of the info I got from the team:

1. Jennifer O'Rourke: Grade 12, team captain, cute as a button and twice as smart. She was the team's history and literature expert.
2. Maximillian Stromopolous: Grade 11, tall, dark and dour. The guy looked like he hadn't cracked a smile since first grade. He was the science expert.
3. Peggi Miggs: Grade 11, wound as tight as a mob snitch in prison. She was the math expert.
4. Lisa Aucoin: Grade 10, small and mousy with bad case of chronic halitosis. She was the team alternate.

They all agreed that the last time they saw Tobias was when he left school on Tuesday at five p.m., just after their team practice. His grandfather picked Tobias up in his car and, as far as they knew, drove Tobias home.

"Do you have any suspects in mind?" I asked, looking around the table.

"Suspects?" they mumbled, their eyebrows raised in unison.

"Yeah," I said, "anyone who might hold a grudge against Tobias?"

There was a short pause while the girls twiddled their thumbs. Max, however, was glaring at me like I'd just insulted his sister, mother and grandmother all at once. Most people get nervous when somebody stares at them like that. Me, I just get interested. That's when Jennifer broke the tension.

"May we speak in private?" she said, standing up.

"I don't know, Jennifer," I said. "I think Max has something he wants to get off his chest."

"This is ridiculous," Max said, standing up and switching his icy glare from me to Jennifer. "This is utterly ridiculous!" Then he stalked away. Lisa Aucoin sprang up and chased after him. Peggi Miggs just stayed right where she was and looked confused.

"Please, Jack," Jennifer said, taking me by the arm. "Let him go. He's just upset because we've decided to bring the case to you rather than get Principal Snit involved."

"I'll let it go for now," I said, and I let her guide me to a more private table at the back of the cafeteria. "But Max better watch himself. He doesn't know who he's messing with."

"Forget Max," she said. Then she leaned in and whispered, "I suppose Valda Pernickle may still harbor some feelings of animosity toward Tobias."

"Valda Pernickle?" I asked. That name sounded more made up than a girl on her way to the prom.

"His ex-girlfriend," she said. "They had a messy breakup. She blames the Academic All-Stars Trivia Tournament."

"And you actually think this girl is capable of kidnapping Tobias?"I asked with a smirk.

"You don't know Valda," she said, without an ounce of humor.

"Is there anyone else?" I asked.

She shook her head. "I don't think so."

"I'll see what I can find out."

"And remember, Jack, we need him back before tomorrow night," she added, as we stood up. "Before the Regional Final starts."

"What time is that?"

"Seven."

"Then I'll need two things. First, give me your number so I can get in touch with you. Second, show me where Valda's locker is. I'll need to ask her a few questions."

Thursday, March 12, 12:43 p.m.
Iona High, Locker 225

Jennifer gave me her number and took me up to Valda's locker. Jennifer's hair smelled like pink cotton candy, and she had a cute way of talking out of the side of her mouth. I thought I could get hooked on a girl like her if I wasn't careful, and I wasn't planning on being careful.

Valda's locker was in the science wing on the second floor. I said my good-byes to Jennifer and took up a position a couple of yards away from the locker. I casually leaned against the wall, pretending to look over a chemistry quiz

I'd found on the ground, while the hallway filled up with students coming back from lunch. Mixed in with the crowd was a tall dame with pale skin and jet-black hair who stepped up to Locker 225. She wore a scowl that made her look like a red-hot poker, and I wasn't crazy about burning my hands. But I had a job to do, and I wasn't going to let a Sour Sally like Valda get in my way.

"Valda Pernickle," I said, stepping over to her locker.

"What?" she barked, giving me a quick once-over.

"I was wondering if you know anything about the possible whereabouts of Tobias Poe."

"I have no idea where Toby is," she said with a sneer. "And I really don't care. I haven't thought about him since we broke up seventeen days ago. And who are you to be asking me personal questions, anyway?"

"My name is Jack Lime, and I'm trying to track him down," I said.

"Well, I don't want to talk about him, Jack Lime," she said, fiddling with her combination lock.

I decided to try turning on the old charm instead of playing it straight up. "I'm sorry if I caught you at a bad time, Valda, and I'm sure an attractive young lady like yourself is better off without Tobias. But I need to find him, so if you could give me any information, I'd be forever in your debt."

"I know I'm better off without him. I've never been happier, but I really don't know where he is," she said, pulling on the lock. It still wouldn't open, so she started spinning the dial again.

"Is there anywhere in particular he used to go to get away from things? Somewhere he'd go to be alone? Somewhere he might go to hide?"

"Without Tobias holding me back, I can date anyone I want. I can go on a date every night of the week," she said, trying the lock again. It still wouldn't open. "What was your name again?"

"Jack," I said. This conversation was getting dangerously off track. "Valda, is there anywhere Tobias would go to get away from things?"

Valda quit with the lock and turned to face me. Her expression went from irritated to fascinated faster than you can say Attention Deficit Disorder.

"What did you say?" she asked.

"Is there anywhere Tobias would go to get away from things?"

"His study."

"His study?"

"He calls it his study, but it's really just an old shed in his backyard. But enough about Toby," she said, leaning in. "I don't think we've ever met before, have we, Jack?"

"No," I said. "I just moved here."

"You're the new boy from California," she said, sliding even closer to me. "They were right."

"About what?"

"You *are* cute."

"Ah ... yes ... well," I mumbled, inching away from her. "I don't suppose you could give me Tobias's address?"

"Thirteen Oort Cloud Court," she said in a husky whisper. "More important, Jack, what's *your* address?"

"Say, it's been a real treat talking to you, Valda," I said, and tried to make a polite exit. "Thanks for the tip on the study. I'll be sure to check that out."

"Wait," she said, grabbing my arm. "Could you just hold my books while I open my locker?"

Before I could think of a reason why I had to leave immediately, she threw her backpack into my arms. It weighed a ton. If this girl could lug around a bag that heavy, she might actually be able to overpower a brainiac like Tobias and lock him in a closet.

"Thanks," she said, popping open her locker. What I saw made me a little scared, and a whole lot suspicious. Valda's locker was wallpapered with pictures of herself and a boy; he was a little shorter than her, heavyset but not fat, with curly brown hair and glasses. "Is that Tobias?" I asked.

"Whoops," she said, slamming the door shut. "I haven't had a chance to take those down yet, but Toby doesn't mean a thing to me anymore, Jack." She grabbed my arm. "My, you're strong aren't you?"

"Not strong enough to hold this bag much longer," I said. "What's in here, anyway? A dead body?" As soon as the words left my mouth, I wanted to take them back, but Valda didn't blink.

"I'm sorry it's so heavy, but I read a lot of books," she said, batting her eyelashes. "What I really need is more dating, less reading, don't you think?"

"Right," I said. "Well, I need to get going ..." I couldn't think of a logical way to get out of this intimate little conversation, so I put the bag down and started backing away.

"Come back anytime," she said, and waved good-bye with her index finger.

"You bet," I said, and made a quick exit down the hall.

Thursday, March 12, 4:07 p.m.
52 Katana Boulevard, The Mist

I decided it'd be best to investigate Toby's shed under the cover of darkness. Folks in Iona don't take kindly to kids snooping around in their backyards in the middle of the afternoon, and Jennifer had made me promise to keep this investigation quiet. Plus, I had another hunch I wanted to follow. Max Stromopolous was the only person on the team who had got all twisted up about me getting involved in the case. The way I figured it, Max might have been miffed that he wasn't the top dog on the team and wanted to get rid of Tobias so he could have the spotlight. It was just a hunch, but I decided it was worth looking into. Plus, it gave me an excuse to call Jennifer.

"Jack," she said, once I explained what I was thinking. "I understand that you're the professional, but I believe you are wasting your time investigating Max."

"Thanks for the concern, doll, but any gumshoe worth his salt will follow all the leads before crossing any suspects off his list."

"Am I on that list, Jack?" she asked.

"Did you kidnap Tobias?" I asked.

"No," she said.

"That's good enough for me," I said, and I could hear her smiling on the other end.

"I guess you have to do what you feel is right, Jack," she said. "But don't press Max too much. He's very sensitive."

"I bet he is," I said. "Now how about that address?"

Jennifer gave me Max's address and apartment number. He lived in a luxury condominium complex called The Mist on the main drag in The Steppes. If you've never had the pleasure of visiting The Steppes, Doc, it's a lot like wandering into Beverly Hills; the houses get a whole lot bigger, and the fences get a whole lot higher. Naming the place The Mist was in keeping with the mysterious quality Luxemcorp was trying to build around their highfalutin' neighborhood.

I stepped into the main foyer and was about to buzz up when I noticed a nice old lady loaded down with grocery bags coming up the front walk. I decided to improvise.

"I can help you with those, ma'am," I said, flashing her my pearly whites.

"Thank you, young man," she said, handing me the bags.

"No problem at all," I said. "I was on my way up to visit a friend anyway. Now I can surprise him." Did I feel good about lying to a nice old lady? No, but when opportunity knocks, you've got to answer the door. Plus, it's not like she didn't get anything out of the deal. She didn't have to lug a bunch of heavy bags up to her condo, and it gave her the chance to hang out with a handsome young man. She thanked me for my hard work with a homemade chocolate chip cookie.

I ate my cookie and made my way up to the penthouse suite. The door was a big, wide piece of dark wood that looked heavy and thick. There was no peephole in the middle (that would probably ruin the aesthetics), which was a bonus, since I didn't want to have this conversation through the door anyway. There was no bell, so I did things the old-fashioned way: I knocked.

After a short wait, the door opened, but only a crack.

"Lime," Max said, peeking out. "What are you doing here?"

When I met Max in the cafeteria, he came across as tall, dark and dour. Nothing had changed. He still looked as grim as a nuclear scientist at a reactor meltdown. The way he kept the security chain fastened told me he wasn't going to invite me in for a warm cup of tea. The cool reception made me think Max might be my man after all.

"I just have a few questions for you, Max," I said, trying to seem as friendly as possible.

"I don't have time for questions," he said.

A voice, a distinctly female voice, called from inside the condo. "Who is it, Max?"

"No one," Max said, without turning around.

"That hurts, Max," I said. "I don't suppose you'd mind telling me who's in there with you?"

"Yeah, I would mind, actually," he said.

"We can play it that way if you want, Max," I said, taking a step toward the door. "But you're only making things harder on yourself. If you've got nothing to hide, I can be a real sweet guy. But if I find out you've been holding back on me, Max, I'm going to come down on you like a hammer on an anvil."

Max opened his mouth to say something, then stopped and just closed the door. I heard the deadbolt click and knew that our interview was over. But I wasn't quite done with Max. I needed to find out who was in there with him, and I was willing to wait.

I strolled down the hall toward the elevators. The great thing about classy places like The Mist is that they always have perks, like places to sit while you wait for the elevator to arrive. In this case, it was a neat little nook with a comfortable pleather chair. They even had a copy of the day's paper to read.

While I waited, I flipped through the paper, but I was too busy keeping my eyes peeled for Max's female friend to pay much attention to what I was reading. That is, until I got to page three. There, in black and white, was a story about the big Academic All-Stars trivia match between Iona High and Montgomery Academy. It turns out Montgomery was a prestigious private school, jam-packed with the best and brightest our slice of the world has to offer. They were three-time defending champions. Iona High was touted as the new kid on the block that was set to dethrone the old guard. The journalist who had written the piece had interviewed Jennifer and had quoted her as saying that Tobias was the main reason they'd made it to the finals. There was no mention of Max or any of the other people on the team, which I was sure would have added fuel to Max's fire. I was just starting to read about Montgomery Academy when a small, mousy girl marched past me and down the stairs. It was Lisa Aucoin, the team alternate.

I tailed her, making sure I kept my distance until she was clear of the front door. I didn't want her scurrying back to take refuge in Max's arms.

"Lisa," I called, when she'd reached the edge of the parking lot. "Could I have a word with you?"

"I'm too busy right now," she said, picking up the pace.

"Then, why don't we walk and talk?" I asked, practically breaking into a jog.

"We don't have anything to talk about," she said, trying hard not to look at me.

I cut to the chase. "Is Tobias at Max's?"

"No," she said, putting on the brakes. "Of course not."

"And I suppose Max doesn't know squat about his whereabouts?"

"I'd know if Max had anything to do with Tobias's disappearance because we're ..." she started, and then caught herself. But it was too late. The cat was out of the bag.

"Because you two lovebirds are an item," I said. It wasn't a question.

"We're just getting ready for tomorrow night," she said, but the red patches that suddenly blossomed on her cheeks told me otherwise.

"Of course," I said. "And now that Tobias is out of the way, you'll be center stage instead of watching from the sidelines."

"Well, I didn't *kidnap* him, if that's what you're implying," she said, and started to walk away again.

"Getting a shot at the limelight is a pretty good motive," I said, following along.

"Look, Jack, I deserve to be on that team. Everybody

knows it. In practice, I consistently score higher than anyone else. But I'm in Grade 10, so I have to wait my turn."

"You're telling me that you can beat Tobias?"

"Definitely," she said, like I'd just figured out that two plus two equals four.

"I'm sorry, Lisa, but I find that hard to believe."

"Believe whatever you want," she said, picking up the pace again.

"So maybe Max did it," I said. "With Tobias out of the way, there'd be room for his secret girlfriend on the team. Plus, he wouldn't have to play Robin to Tobias's Batman in front of the whole school."

"First of all, I'm not his secret girlfriend. Second, Max isn't anyone's sidekick, especially not Tobias's," she said and then broke into a sprint.

"So where do you think he is?" I asked, grabbing her arm. I'd had it with this traveling interrogation.

"I don't know," she said, yanking her arm out of my hand. "I don't know if he went on a vacation, or the other team took him, or if the boys running the silly betting pool locked him away to mess around with the odds. I don't have a clue. That's why Jennifer hired you, isn't it? To find him? She's the only one who cares if he makes it to the match tomorrow night anyway."

Lisa stormed away, but I didn't care. Alarm bells were going off in my head.

Thursday, March 12, 4:45 p.m.
A street with no name, Grandma's House

The case and all its angles had me twisted up. I certainly hadn't eliminated the possibility that Max and Lisa were playing me for a chump and had Tobias tied up in Max's fancy condo, but a numbers racket put a whole new spin on things.

If Lisa wasn't just cracking foxy, then a betting pool would be a big lead. Not only would the ringleaders have reason to kidnap Tobias, but they'd be exactly the kind of wingnuts who would pull a stunt like this. What I needed to do was find a way to get on the inside of this betting ring and crack it wide open. That's what I was thinking about when I started up my grandma's front walk, so I didn't notice Valda Pernickle sitting on the porch.

"Hi, Jack," she said, bounding down the walk toward me.

"Valda," I said, ready to make a run for it. "What are you doing here?"

"I wanted to see how your investigation was going."

"How long have you been here? Where's my grandma?"

"I've only been here for about an hour," she said. "Your grandma's inside. She invited me to stay for supper. Isn't that great? I can't wait to hear all about your day." She grabbed my arm and started dragging me toward the door.

In my former life, my mom and dad used to make things like steamed salmon on wild rice for dinner. Or we might have pad thai with a glass of mango lassi on the side. I hated to admit it, because I considered myself a bit of a sophisticated city slicker, but none of that stuff compared to my grandma's meatloaf, and Thursday was meatloaf night. Unfortunately, the meatloaf didn't taste quite as good with

Valda staring across the table at me like a cougar on the prowl.

"So tell us all about your day, Jack," Valda said, while I plowed food into my mouth. I figured if I could eat fast, I might be able to get out of this ambush without getting hurt too badly.

"Not much to tell," I said, in between hunks of meatloaf.

"Oh, I'm sure a detective like you must have lots of interesting things to tell us," Valda said, reaching her foot under the table and rubbing my calf. I jerked away and accidentally flung a spoonful of potatoes at my grandma's face. Luckily, Grandma is quick for her age, and the potatoes ended up on the wall behind her.

"You're awfully jumpy, Jack," Grandma said, scooping the potatoes off the wall.

"Sorry about that," I said, getting up. "Let me throw those out."

"Nonsense," she said. "You stay here and talk to your friend ... and try to relax."

Once Grandma was out of earshot, Valda leaned across the table with a crazy look in her eyes. I thought she was going to try to smooch me, but she only wanted to talk. "Jack," she said, in a low voice, "I wanted to tell you that there are people betting on the game tomorrow night. I heard them talking about fixing it so Montgomery would win. They think they're going to make a fortune. Do you think that might have something to do with Tobias's disappearance?"

"I already know about the betting pool, Valda," I said, looking pained and rubbing my temples. The last thing

I wanted to do was let Valda think she could get involved in my investigation, but in reality I could've kissed her. Between Lisa and Valda, this case was starting to shape up. Not only had they confirmed that there was a gambling operation at Iona High, but the fix was in for Montgomery to come out on top. And without Tobias around, it sounded like Iona High was sure to lose.

"You do?" Valda said, looking shocked.

"Lisa Aucoin told me," I said.

She smiled as if this were the greatest news she'd heard in a long time. The girl was as nutty as a slice of pecan pie. Then, as my grandma came back to the table, she sat back in her chair.

"Gee whiz, this is terrific meatloaf, Mrs. Lime," Valda said.

"Thank you, Valda," Grandma said. "It's nice to know someone appreciates my cooking enough to keep from throwing it on the walls."

Thursday, March 12, 9:12 p.m.
Grandma's House, My Room

Valda ate a lot, and she ate it slowly. Then she stayed for tea and cookies. By the time we'd retired to the living room and she'd started telling us about the spoon collection she'd inherited from her Great Aunt Beatrice, I thought even Grandma had had enough of her. An hour later, we managed to nudge Valda out the door. I hightailed it up the stairs, and when I was safely barricaded in my room, I gave Jennifer a call.

"Hi, Jack," she said, in her bubbly way. "Did you find Tobias?"

"Not yet," I said, "but I will. Don't worry about that."

"But you've got some leads, right?"

"I have a few leads," I admitted. "Say, do you know anything about people betting on the match?"

"Yes," she groaned. "There are a couple of guys on the football team who are running some kind of pool, but they're just fooling around. They think this is all a big joke. But the last time I checked, the football team didn't make it to the regional finals."

"Do you know anyone I could talk to about placing a bet?"

"You don't think they're mixed up with Tobias's disappearance, do you?"

"I don't think so, but I have to follow the lead."

"I know somebody who might be able to act as a liaison for us, Jack. Why don't we meet tomorrow morning in the cafeteria? Is eight-twenty all right?"

"Sure," I said, before hanging up. "And don't worry about breakfast, it's on me."

All in all, it was a productive night. I'd managed to find out that the gambling operation was more than just a curve ball that Lisa had thrown my way to keep the heat off her and Max. I was a step closer to a meeting with one of the hoods involved in that numbers racket. And more often than not, where there's a numbers racket, there are grifters and con-men hanging around like vultures after a fresh kill. But I had a whole night before I could follow that lead, and I wanted to tie up a loose end that was still eating away at me.

It was time to take a closer look at Tobias's Fortress of Solitude: his shed.

Thursday, March 12, 10:37 p.m.
Grandma's House, The Garage

Thanks to Valda's ridiculously long visit, my grandma was not in a good mood. I'd never heard her grumble about anything before, but she grumbled all the way up the stairs, she grumbled while she brushed her teeth, and she grumbled when she got into bed. She didn't stop grumbling until she started snoring at ten-fifteen, and even then, her snores sounded angrier than normal. I stuck around until ten-thirty, then I figured I could slip out of the house without waking her up.

I grabbed the flashlight my grandma keeps in the towel closet, plus the key to the garage, and headed outside. Back before Iona was sold lock, stock and barrel to Luxemcorp Inc., my grandpa was the town carpenter and all-round handyman, so the garage is actually more like a small barn that's jam-packed with tools from the floor to the ceiling. After a lot of stumbling around in the dark, a few nasty bumps and a couple of choice words, I found the crowbar I was looking for and headed outside. That's when I bumped into Valda Pernickle.

"Valda, what do you think you're doing?" I hissed.

"Where're you going, Jack?" she said, stepping closer to me.

"I just need to do some work for the case," I said, stepping back. I felt a headache coming on.

"That's exciting," she squealed. "Can I come? Please?"

"Gee, that would be great, Valda," I said, squeezing the crowbar, "but I think I need to go alone. Two people on a delicate job like this is definitely one too many."

"Where are you going?" she said, stepping up and grabbing my hand. "Will it be dangerous?"

"Well, Valda," I said, feeling the weight of the crowbar in my hand, "let's put it this way: if both of us go, then one of us won't live through this night."

"Wow," she said, stepping so close to me that our noses were almost touching. "That is dangerous."

"Very dangerous. Extremely dangerous," I said, twisting my hand free and stepping back again. This time I bumped into the wall of the garage. I had nowhere left to run.

"Be careful, Jack," she said, stepping up again. And then, faster than you can say "sneak attack," she was kissing me square on the lips.

I'm a gentleman, but I couldn't bring myself to kiss her back. That didn't seem to bother her. Once she was done, she stepped back with a sly smile plastered on her face. "I'll see you tomorrow."

And then she disappeared into the darkness of the night.

Thursday, March 12, 10:48 p.m.
13 Oort Cloud Court, The Poe Residence

Valda was clearly insane. The kind of crazy that can really make a guy sweat. But fortunately, it was a cold night, and it didn't take me long to clear her out of my head. It was cold enough for me to wish I'd worn my parka instead of my leather jacket, and cold enough to start wishing for a wool hat halfway to the Poe residence. But there was no time to turn back. My grandma is a very predictable sleeper, and thanks to my constant insomnia, I knew that she'd be up for a trip to the facilities by twelve-thirty; you could set your watch by it.

As you know, Doc, insomnia just means that you can't fall asleep at night, which is a very convenient excuse to stay up late and watch movies. That sounds great for a couple nights, or even a week, but it gets old pretty fast. Especially when all you want to do is grab a couple of hours of shut-eye to clear the cobwebs out of your head.

So, I had just under two hours to get the job done and slip back into bed. If Grandma happened to peek into my room and I wasn't there, I'd be grounded until I was ready to leave for college.

I slunk onto the Poe property via the neighbor's garden and decided to suss out the place from behind a short evergreen. From there, I was pretty sure that I could see weak beams of light creeping out from the cracks of the shed's front door. I have to admit that I got a little excited, and I started toward the shed without thinking things through. It was an amateur move, and I paid the price. I'd only managed to take nine or ten steps before a security light flicked on from the side of the Poe house, illuminating the entire backyard. I froze for a second and then made a beeline for the shed. I hugged the side wall and crept behind the shed, where I figured I was hidden from the light's sensors. After a minute of me standing like a statue, the lights went out, and I started moving again.

Luckily, there was a small window at about head height on the shed's back wall. It was frosted and I couldn't see in, but I could tell it was pitch black inside. The light I'd seen coming out of the front door was either wishful thinking on my part, or the floodlight had warned Tobias that someone was coming and he'd made things get dark PDQ.

I jimmied the thin edge of the crowbar into the frame of the window and applied pressure. First there was a high-pitched creak, and then a loud pop as the metal latch on the inside snapped off. I slid the window open, flicked on my flashlight and scanned the shed. It was dark inside, but I could see enough to know that Valda hadn't been joking; Tobias had transformed the joint into a nice little study. Along the right wall was a sturdy-looking bookcase that stretched from the back to the front of the shed and reached from the floor to the ceiling. It was packed with books. On the left side, a whiteboard had been screwed into the wall. It was covered in grids and tables, each one filled with numbers. I figured Tobias must've been practicing his math. Directly below the window was a wooden desk. On it was a closed laptop and a stack of textbooks. Other than that, the shed was empty. I turned the flashlight off, stuck it in my pocket and hoisted myself up.

Once I was inside, I turned the flashlight on and scanned the room. The bookcase and whiteboard weren't telling me much, so I took a closer look at the laptop. When I popped the cover open, I was surprised to discover that not only was it still on but there was a spreadsheet minimized in the taskbar. I opened it. Like the whiteboard, the spreadsheet was covered with meaningless tables, each filled with numbers, with titles like VBCham, or FB1, or AATT. It was probably some convoluted physics calculation. But I was curious about when this work had been done. I clicked on the *File* button at the top of the page, then *Properties*, and saw that the spreadsheet had been modified only twenty-three minutes ago. Tobias must've been in here after all, but the security light had tipped him off. So where was he? Did he sneak out the front while I was coming in the back? I didn't think he could have escaped without me hearing something. I gave another look around the room. There was nowhere to hide except —

I stepped over to the bookcase and ran my fingers over the books. They looked real enough, but close up, I found out they were just the spines of dead books pasted onto a series of long panels. The entire wall was a fake. I guesstimated there were probably three or four feet of space behind the panels where Tobias could be hiding, which explained how he could disappear so quickly. There must've been a secret door somewhere, but I didn't have the patience to find it. It was time to end this charade, and I was just about to let him know the game was up when an interesting thought popped into my head: Valda and Jennifer had both mentioned that some lowbrow gamblers were betting against Iona to win because Tobias was missing, and they were planning on winning a pile of geetus. But what if Tobias showed up at the last minute? And what if you were the only one who knew he'd be making it to the big game? Seemed to me, if I played this right, I could solve this case and stand to make a tidy bundle of dough on the side. I just needed to make sure Toby didn't get nervous and fly the coop before I got back tomorrow afternoon to drag him back to school.

"Hello, Jennifer, it's Jack," I said loudly, pretending to be on the phone. "I guess Tobias isn't here after all. I'll have to let everyone know that he's still missing, and that he's definitely not in his shed." I was hedging my bets that my public service announcement would be enough to convince a Nervous Nellie like Tobias to stay put. This was risky business, but Risk happened to be my middle name. The chumps at Iona High just didn't know it yet.

Or that's what I thought, Doc. Little did I know that greed, stupid greed, would be my downfall.

Friday, March 13, 8:02 a.m.
Iona High, The Cafeteria

As it turned out, my grandma didn't have to use the facilities until nearly four in the a.m. I know, because I couldn't sleep. I was busy figuring out how much spinach I could earn on this Academic All-Stars gambit. I was confident that a high roller from the City of Angels like myself could walk away with a suitcase full of cash playing in the little leagues of Iona. So I had a little swagger in my step when I walked into the cafeteria that morning carrying two cinnamon buns and two large coffees. I was just about to sit down when Jennifer walked in with a lanky hipster wearing baggy jeans and a sideways baseball cap.

"Hi, Jack," she said, flashing one of her adorable smiles. "This is Mike."

"What up?" Mike said, nodding his head to a silent beat and scanning the empty cafeteria.

"I got you a cinnamon bun and a coffee," I said to Jennifer. "I hope you take sugar and cream."

"Sorry," she said. "I don't drink coffee. It makes me anxious."

"No problem," I said. "I'll have yours, too. I need as much caffeine as I can get. I had a late night."

"Did you find —" she started, but I broke in before she could bring up Tobias. The last thing I needed was for Mike to know I had the inside scoop on the whereabouts of the missing trivia superstar.

"... the book I lost? Yes, I found it," I said with a wink.

"Really?" she said, practically jumping up and down.

"Chill, Jenny," Mike said, coming out of his daze. "It's just a book."

"It's an important book," I said. "A very important book. But we're not here to talk about books. We're here to talk about something more interesting, aren't we, Mike?"

"Right on," Mike said with a grin.

"Why don't you take a load off and enjoy your cinnamon bun while Mike and I go talk shop," I said to Jennifer, holding out a chair. "I assume cinnamon doesn't make you anxious, too."

"Of course not," she said, taking the bun, "but you'd better come back and fill me in on that book you found."

"It's a deal," I said, then turned to Mike. "Do you mind if we walk and talk?"

"Let's do it," Mike said, and we went for a stroll.

Friday, March 13, 8:11 a.m.
Iona High, The Main Foyer

"So, Mike," I said, acting casual, "what're the odds on the match tonight?"

"Used to be, when Tobias was around, Iona had two-to-one odds to win. But that all changed when he disappeared."

"So now it's two-to-one that Montgomery wins?"

"Three-to-one, actually," he said.

"That means if I bet ten bucks on Iona, and they win, I'd get thirty bucks?" I asked, pretending I didn't have a sweet clue how betting odds worked.

"That's right," Mike said, and then he whipped out a little black book from his back pocket. "So how much can I put you down for?"

"One hundred bucks," I said, expecting this guy's jaw to hit the ground when he heard a number that big being thrown around.

Instead all I got was a frown. "That's not very much," he said.

It was very much in my books, but I wasn't going to let a two-bit crook like Mike know that.

"Well, how does two hundred sound, smart guy?" I said.

"Ah," Mike grimaced. "I guess that's all right for a first-timer."

"First-timer?" I said, with a chuckle. "Kid, you don't know who you're messing with." Sure, it might've been my first time dealing with that kind of dough, but I'd laid down a few bets in my time. Why just that past summer, Chuck Smith and I had been laying down quarters on Dodgers' games, so it's not like I didn't know what I was doing. I reminded myself that I was in the driver's seat on this one; after all, I was the only one who had the inside scoop on the whereabouts of Tobias Poe.

"Well, heck, Mike, I was worried that I might break the bank if I started throwing around some big numbers, but I guess you guys are the real deal. So how about we say six hundred clams. How's that tickle your funny bone?"

"You sure you want to put down that much?"

"What's the matter, Mike? Can't handle it?"

"I'll have to check with the boss," he said, slipping the little black book into his back pocket and pulling out his cell. He dialed, turned away and whispered some mumbo-jumbo into the phone. When he was done squawking to his boss, he handed the phone over.

"Are you Lime?" the big boss asked, in a voice that was deep and threatening. Whoever was on the other end was trying hard to scare me off.

"That's right," I said.

"Six hundred bucks is a lot of cash. How do I know you're good for it?"

I pulled a wad of dough out of my pocket and counted it quickly. "I've got ninety bucks on me and the rest in the bank." (FYI — This was a lie. I'd been spending my allowance from the trust account like it was going out of style. I might have had fifty bucks in the bank on top of the ninety in my hand, but he didn't need to know that, and I didn't plan on losing.) "But if you're worried, I'll put up my cell and my iPod. You can use those for collateral if I lose."

I was trying to rope this yahoo into my bet, and I was expecting him to accept that kind of an offer in good faith. Instead, all I got was the silent treatment, and I'm not a big fan of the silent treatment.

"Well, if that's not good enough, bucko," I said, a little perturbed by his distinct lack of enthusiasm, "why don't I throw in my laptop and we can jack up the bet? The laptop's worth at least a grand, so how about we say an even twelve hundred, with the iPod and the cell thrown in for good measure?"

"I think you're getting out of your league," he said.

"You don't know my league, hombre," I said. "But if you can't handle a twelve-hundred-dollar bet, I'll just have to find a new vendor. Do you know anyone who can handle serious bets?"

There was a long pause on the other end before he mumbled, "Twelve hundred dollars is just fine."

"Fine," I said.

"With the laptop, the cell and the iPod as collateral?"

"That's right," I said.

"Put Mike back on the phone," the big boss said. I handed the phone over, and Mike did a lot of nodding and frowning. Then he hung up, whipped out his little black book and a silver pen from his pocket, made a few notes and handed it over to me.

"Just sign at the bottom."

I read the page over. The printing was tiny, but incredibly neat. The long and the short of it was that if Iona lost, I was out my laptop, my cell phone and my iPod if I couldn't pay the twelve hundred dollars within twenty-four hours.

I have to admit, I was feeling a little in over my head, but I couldn't back down, so I signed on the dotted line. What else could I do?

Friday, March 13, 3:42 p.m.
13 Oort Cloud Court, The Poe Residence

Standing outside Tobias's shed, with only a few hours until game time, I was feeling the crunch. Twelve hundred smackers was a heck of a lot of cabbage, and I didn't think Dave (the butter-and-egg man who controls my dough back in Cali) would pump that kind of cash into my account without asking some serious questions. But worrying wasn't going to get me anywhere. I needed to take care of business and get Tobias back to Iona High before the trivia questions started flying and Jennifer found herself on center stage without the team ringer. So as soon as school let out, I made my way to Tobias's house, crept around back and hunkered down below the window. For a few seconds, it was dead quiet, and I was sure he'd found a new place to crash, which meant that yours truly was up the proverbial creek without a proverbial paddle. Then the soft clickety-clack of the keyboard started up, and I could practically smell all that money just on the other side of the shed wall. I stood up and threw the window open.

"Don't move," I yelled.

The poor sap was so surprised he fell backward in his chair, taking the desk down with him. The laptop hit the floor with a crash.

"I said freeze," I yelled again, starting to hoist myself into the shed, but my orders were falling on deaf ears. Tobias was in panic mode, and there was no stopping him now. He scrambled to his feet and flew out the front door.

I bolted around the side of the shed and spotted him running through the neighbor's garden. I plowed along behind him, getting closer and closer with every step. I have to admit, Tobias was fast for a pinhead, but twelve hundred clams is a great motivator. When he came to a shoulder-high fence about four lawns away, the chase was over. He'd just managed to get to the top when I grabbed one foot and yanked him to the ground.

"Don't make me go! Don't make me go!" he was screaming. I pinned him down and waited until he wore himself out.

"Are you through with the kicking and screaming?" I asked.

"I don't want to go," he squealed.

"Well, you're going, tough guy, and there's no way around it. You might be book smart, Tobias, but you don't have any idea how the real world works. This is more than just fun and games. There's more to it than that, bucko, a whole lot more. Now, are you going to come along like a man or a mouse?"

"I won't go," he said, starting to struggle again.

"Tobias, one way or another, you're going back to school and you're going to win Iona that championship banner. We can do this the easy way or the hard way, but we're going to do it, capiche?"

The struggling finally stopped and Tobias nodded. In the end he understood just fine.

Friday, March 13, 6:58 p.m.
Iona High, The Auditorium

Tobias resigned himself to his fate and walked into the auditorium without so much as a peep. Of course, Jennifer was thrilled. As soon as Tobias was settled in his seat, she came down and gave me the kind of hug that could melt a Popsicle in a deep freeze. I wish I could say that hug was the beginning of a wonderful evening, but that would be a lie. Not only was Tobias less than inspiring, he was downright bad. I'd give you the play-by-play, but it doesn't matter in the end; Iona lost by forty points. I got out of there before the dust had settled and went back home. I wasn't avoiding anyone; heck, I knew when it was time to pay the piper. I just wanted some time to think about what I was doing traipsing around town pretending to be some sort of detective instead of delivering newspapers like a regular kid. All that thinking just got me a big fat headache and another long, sleepless night.

Saturday, March 14, 6:09 p.m.
A street with no name, Grandma's House

Mike paid me a visit Saturday evening with a couple of heavies from the football team who waited at the end of the driveway, looking tough. If they thought I was going to kick up a stink, they were dead wrong. I handed over my iPod, my cell and my laptop and said good riddance before they had time to look smug.

Of course, my grandma, who's nobody's fool, found out about the whole fiasco. She made a few quick calls to California and cut off my tidy little allowance faster than you can say poorhouse. From then on, the money would be put into an account for my education. She even threatened to call Principal Snit and let him know that a gambling ring was operating right under his nose at Iona High, but I begged and pleaded with her until she gave up. The last thing I needed was to be known as the school snitch.

I tried to call Jennifer, but she didn't pick up. For some silly reason, I thought talking to her might heal the pain.

Sunday, March 15, 10:37 a.m.
13 Oort Cloud Court, The Shed

On Sunday, I went to pay Tobias a visit. I felt like I owed the poor sucker an apology. I had him pegged for a pretty fragile kid, and I'd put him in a bad situation for my own greedy reasons. So I wanted to let him know that I would back him up if he needed a friend.

I figured he might be holed up in his shed, so that's where I headed. This time, I decided to skip the back window and use the front door. The place was pretty much cleared out; no more desk, no laptop, no textbooks. The whiteboard was still up, and the bookcase was still there, but everything else was gone.

I strolled over to the bookcase and started pushing on the panels, looking for the secret door. When I got to the bottom row, closest to the desk, the panel popped off and I found myself looking down a long narrow room. There were crumbs on the ground, an empty can of Coke, and a few nails and tacks sticking out of the wall with scraps of paper still attached to them. I spotted a small black filing cabinet squeezed into the far end with the drawers still open, so I slithered in to see what I could find. The hanging files inside were all empty, but I spotted a yellow sticky note lying at the bottom of the cabinet that read

Call Mike re football scores.

Call Mike? Was that the same Mike that Jennifer had introduced me to? Why would an egghead like Tobias know a punk like Mike? And if Tobias did know Mike, and he was involved in the gambling ring, then —

That's when a lightbulb went on in my head. It came

on with a white-hot light that made the back of my eyeballs hurt. I slipped back into the main part of the shed and rushed to the whiteboard. One of the grids I'd ignored the other night was titled AATT. Could that stand for Academic All-Stars Trivia Tournament? I looked over the grid. This was no math project; the letters down the side were probably pseudonyms for people who were laying down bets (to protect the identity of the guilty), the numbers were the amounts of each bet and on the top row were the odds. Tobias had been running the gambling operation at Iona High all along! This whole thing had been a setup, and he'd left it all there, right under my nose. I'd been duped, hoodwinked, bamboozled.

Monday, March 16, 8:22 a.m.
Iona High, The Cafeteria

I stormed into Iona High first thing Monday morning looking for Jennifer. I wanted to warn her that Tobias was a wolf in sheep's clothing. I wanted to protect her from getting hurt. But when I stepped into the cafeteria, I realized that she already knew all about Tobias Poe. You see, Doc, she was sitting with him and Valda and Mike.

"Jack! Come on over!" Tobias yelled across the cafeteria when he spotted me. "I have to thank you for the new laptop. Mine was broken when you stormed in on me yesterday. That's my own fault, though. Valda called to let me know you were on your way, but I got caught up adding a few last-minute bets on tonight's basketball game. Say, would you like to place a bet? Maybe you can win a little money back."

Gone was the squealing, sniveling pinhead who was terrified to get up in front of the school. Instead, Tobias was acting like a suave stockbroker celebrating his latest acquisition. "Or if you don't want to do it now, you could always give me a ring on my cell." He paused for a moment and then said, in the same deep, menacing voice I'd heard on Mike's cell phone. "Is this Lime?"

Everything made perfect sense. Tobias was obviously the ringmaster of this dirty three-ring circus. Valda was always popping up at the worst time because she must have been tailing me to let the others know where I was headed. And then there was Jennifer; she was the one who'd come to me in the first place, who'd identified Valda as a possible suspect, who'd tried to talk me out of investigating Max, and who'd set up my meeting with Mike from the betting pool. They'd all been playing me like a fiddle, and I'd been squeaking in all the right places.

"Why'd you do it?" I asked in a hoarse voice that sounded far, far away.

"Do you remember taking some pictures a couple of weeks ago?" Valda asked. "Of a guy named Ryan Morrison kissing a girl, only the girl wasn't his girlfriend?"

"I remember," I said.

"Good," she said, "because I don't want this next bit to confuse you. See, I remember those pictures, too, Jack, because my last name's not Pernickle, it's Morrison. Making any connections yet?"

"And Valda happens to be my girlfriend, Jack," Tobias

added. "So when she needed me to exact some revenge for her little brother on the town's new peeping tom, I was more than willing to oblige."

"It was genius, darling, pure genius," Valda said with a chuckle.

"You're too kind," Tobias said, standing up and bowing slightly. "But really, it was all too easy. I mean, Jack, it wasn't very difficult to pick out your Achilles' heel."

"Was any of it true?" I asked.

"Well," Jennifer started, "we exaggerated some of the details. Tobias doesn't have the top GPA in the school."

"I'm in the top ten, though," Tobias smirked.

"And he wasn't the captain of the robotics team," Jennifer added.

"But I did lead the chess team to the city championships," he said. "I'd love to play you sometime, Jack. You make me feel so clever."

My heart was pounding. I could feel the blood pumping in my temples. I was ready to kill someone, and I didn't care if it was a boy or a girl. Somebody was going to pay, big time. And that's when, for the very first time, my condition kicked in — and I fell asleep.

Friday, September 27, 8:03 p.m.
Iona Hospital, Room 234

"Finding out that the world isn't always what it seems was a hard pill to swallow, Doc. Harder than anything you've ever given me. But when I woke up that day, all by myself in the cafeteria, I vowed I wouldn't let that happen to anyone else. Not if I could help it. So, that's why I'm still in this dirty racket."

"That's a tall tale, Jack," Potter said.

"But it's all true, Doc. And the more I learned, the more I became certain that Tobias was behind a lot of the shady deals that were going on at Iona High, and I vowed to stop him and all of his cronies. But that's a story for another day."

"That's very noble, Jack," Potter said, getting out of his seat. "And I'm sure your parents would be proud." He was halfway out the door when he stopped and turned around. "Just try to keep your nose clear of any fists for a few days. And get some rest."

"You're the doc, Doc."

"See you soon, Jack."

"I doubt it, Doc. I think I'll take it easy for a while, stay on the straight and narrow, maybe take a vacation from this P.I. gig."

"I wouldn't bet on it, Jack. I wouldn't bet on it."

THE END

The names of the people and places haven't been changed to protect the innocent. Everything is exactly as it happened.

Exploits of a Reluctant (But Extremely Goodlooking) Hero

"This story is sure to appeal to teens who like their narrators edgy, quirky, outrageous, and hilarious."

— School Library Journal

Exploits of a Reluctant (But Extremely Goodlooking) Hero is a novel of adventure, intrigue, Ukrainian dance lessons, disruptive horseplay, inappropriate ogling and some truly heroic consumption of junk food. A hilarious trip into the inner world of a boy teetering on the brink of manhood.

Exploits of a Reluctant (But Extremely Goodlooking) Hero
Written by Maureen Fergus
PB 978-1-55453-025-0

Also by Maureen Fergus

Recipe for Disaster

Francie was born to bake and dreams of one day starring in her own baking show. Her life is almost perfect — until a new girl shows up at school.

Recipe for Disaster
Written by Maureen Fergus
HCJ 978-1-55453-319-0
PB 978-1-55453-320-6